SISTER, SISTER

ANDREW NEIDERMAN

BERKLEY BOOKS, NEW YORK

SISTER, SISTER

A Berkley Book / published by arrangement with
the author

PRINTING HISTORY
Berkley edition / January 1992

ISBN: 0-425-12846-6

PRINTED IN THE UNITED STATES OF AMERICA

10 9 8 7 6 5 4 3 2 1

THEY WERE THE CLOSEST SISTERS ON EARTH. AND NO ONE COULD EVER COME BETWEEN THEM . . .

Not Mary Jessup, the psychologist who choked to death before their very eyes.

Not Mrs. Gerhart, the cook who was electrocuted while the girls watched television.

Not even Neil Richards, their new teacher who had worked with special children before . . .

Because Alpha and Beta are twice as special. And twice as deadly.

Sister, Sister

Don't miss these terrifying novels by Andrew Neiderman . . .

Playmates
In a backwoods farmhouse, a mother and daughter are "adopted" by a strange, demented family.

Surrogate Child
The young boy resembled their dead son so much, it was absolutely creepy . . . and definitely fatal.

Perfect Little Angels
The children of Elysian Fields don't curse, drink, or smoke. They're the perfect teenagers. Perfectly *horrifying*.

Bloodchild
Baby has such sharp teeth . . . and Mommy is so pale and weak, as if she's being bled dry.

AVAILABLE FROM THE BERKLEY PUBLISHING GROUP

For Sammy
Who was the brother I never had

SISTER,
SISTER

Prologue

The nurse standing beside Dr. Henderson turned expectantly as the woman on the stretcher was wheeled into the delivery room. Henderson, on the other hand, didn't even look up from his tray of surgical instruments. The orderly stopped just after closing the door behind himself and waited, staring at the white sheet that hung down from the ceiling in the center of the room.

"Thank you," the nurse said. "That will be all."

The orderly looked at the woman on the stretcher. He knew her water had broken and her contractions were seconds apart, yet neither Dr. Henderson nor the nurse seemed in any particular hurry.

He nodded and left, but he was not a half dozen feet down the hallway before he heard the door being locked behind him. He stopped, looked back at the maternity room, and shrugged. The whole thing was weird anyway. Why did the research center have a separate maternity wing apart from the one in the hospital? Were there some special complications involving this pregnancy?

He didn't ask any questions. They paid him significantly more than he might have gotten elsewhere not to be curious, to obey orders and to forget. People wanted their privacy, he supposed. There were unmarried women or teenagers. When he thought about it, there were a number of reasons to keep a delivery secret. Maybe the babies were sold right after they were born here, and maybe the process wasn't exactly on the up and up. So what? What business was it of his as long as the good check kept coming every two weeks?

He hurried on.

In the maternity room, the nurse wheeled the woman around so her feet faced the sheet. She pushed her into the sheet until the sheet was draped over her abdomen, making it impossible for her to see her lower body.

Dr. Henderson gave her a shot for the pain, then calmly walked around to proceed with the delivery. It did not go smoothly. The woman found herself in a terrible struggle; her eyes bulged with the effort. She had given birth before, but it was nothing like this. Even though the pain was dulled, she screamed in anticipation.

The nurse came around and wiped her forehead without speaking. The woman looked up at her, longing for some sign of compassion, some soothing words, but the nurse was all business. She went right back to assisting Dr. Henderson and the delivery continued.

The woman wasn't really sure when it ended. She sensed a baby emerging, but she still felt great pressure. Then, suddenly she heard the baby's cry.

It was confusing; it was as if the baby cried in stereo. She stared at the white sheet before her, waiting for them to pull it away to show her what she had, but they didn't and the shot Dr. Henderson gave her made her feel groggy now. The pressure eased. She felt herself being stitched quickly, and closed her eyes to wait.

Moments later, the nurse came around to pull her away from the sheet. She looked up expectantly, half smiling, happy it was over, but still a little frightened. The nurse was expressionless.

"What was it?" she asked. The nurse didn't respond. She continued to pull her toward the door. The woman tried to sit up, but the nurse put her hand on her head and forced her back down.

"Relax," she said and unlocked the door.

"But what was it?" she repeated.

"What do you care?" the nurse responded and took her out of the delivery room.

She looked back, but all she saw was the white sheet.

1

After Dr. Sanford Endermo finished his initial description of the project, he tapped the bowl of his cherrywood pipe gently on the side of the large, sea-blue, ceramic ashtray on his desk. It looked like the kind made by mental patients in handicraft class—an awkward, rough circle unevenly painted. Then he sat back in his thick, black leather swivel chair and smiled.

A warmth came into Dr. Endermo's dark, pecan-brown eyes and the lines in his face softened. Neil Richards relaxed again. There was something about the doctor's posture and the brush of gray through his licorice-black hair that gave him an immediate look of self-confidence and authority without a hint of arrogance. He looked fatherly, stable, strong. Neil couldn't help thinking about his own father. He was happy Dr. Endermo had put him at ease.

It was only natural that Neil would feel nervous about coming here to discuss the possibilities of such a bizarre assignment. *This section of the hospital with its security guards, fenced-in areas, and long, quiet, empty corridors would make any-one tense,* he thought. Not that he was the queasy type. Far from it. All this was just quite a change from the public school environment he had been accustomed to, with its crowded, brightly lit, noisy hallways that sometimes bordered on pure bedlam when the students changed classes. There was an energy there that affected him the moment he entered the building.

But here, it was as if . . . as if the building had been quickly abandoned. As if someone had pressed an air raid alert or a fire alarm and everyone was gone. He couldn't help reacting to the deserted look of the place. Dr. Endermo, however, appeared to anticipate all this. Obviously he understood how newcomers reacted. Neil sensed the man was mak-ing a conscious effort to make him feel relaxed.

"Excuse my lab coat," he had told Neil when they first met. "I'm so used to the uniform, I forget I'm wearing it sometimes. I once left this place and went home wearing it. Can you imagine the look on my wife's face when I came in the door? She said, 'What is this, a house call?'"

Neil had laughed and taken the seat Dr. En-dermo had offered him. After Endermo had sat behind his desk, they had stared at one another for a long moment. Then the doctor leaned forward like a man who had concluded it was time to tell the truth. Neil's eyes had widened with interest and Dr. Endermo had begun.

When Dr. Endermo paused now to empty his pipe, Neil sat back and shook his head, naturally finding it difficult to accept the things Dr. Endermo had been telling him, especially because it was Dr. Endermo who had done the talking. The man looked more like a laid-back, old-fashioned country physician than the head of an experimental section in a research center. His hair wasn't wild, his eyes weren't glazed, and he was far from distracted and impersonal.

"I realize," Dr. Endermo went on, "that this is a great deal for you, for any layman that is, to take in at once, but there is just no way to ease into something like this. I hope my detailed descriptions aren't scaring you off."

Neil smiled gently, his blue eyes dancing with an innocent warmth most women found attractive. Like Dr. Endermo, he was a dark-skinned man, but his complexion gave him the appearance of always being tan. He had short, light-brown wavy hair, very neatly trimmed. In fact, dressed in his Pierre Cardin, dark-gray, wide lapel sports jacket, light-gray tie and slacks, and Alexander Julian dress shirt with its button-down collar, he looked more like a Wall Street broker than a twenty-six-year-old special education teacher.

The innocence in his cerulean eyes was offset by the strength and maturity suggested in his sharp, but strong jawbone. There was something rugged in his firm cheek lines and tight, masculine lips. Partly because of his experience with handicapped children and his training in special education, he had a tendency to look intently at people. Women often mistook it for a sexy gaze. It was his intellectual curiosity, however, that made him so visually aggressive.

"I feel as if I'm discussing the plot of a *Twilight Zone* story, or some similar science fiction program."

"Yes, I know what you mean," Dr. Endermo said, a note of sympathetic understanding in his voice. "I must confess, I often feel the same way, even now, even after being involved so long. I suppose that's the charm of working on something as unique as this . . . it never loses its element of fascination." He leaned forward again, but this time his voice filled with an excitement and an enthusiasm that stimulated Neil's own taste for adventure. "I feel like I'm on the brink of some major discovery concerning human behavior. It's equivalent to landing on the moon, if you know what I mean." He sat back and shook his head. "I guess I sound a little overwhelmed with myself and our work sometimes. Sorry."

"Nothing to apologize for," Neil said quickly. "I'm sure I would be the same way about it if I had been in on it right from the start. Your enthusiasm's understandable."

Endermo nodded and put his cleaned pipe in the top right pocket of his lab coat as he sat back in the cloth and leather desk chair, his hands clasped behind his head.

"Not to my wife," he said smiling and shaking his head. "She thinks I've made this office my primary residence," he added and lifted his hands away from his head to indicate the large, light maple paneled room.

It did look like a home office, Neil thought. Although the large, dark-oak desk was covered with papers, an ashtray, a beautiful gold-plated pen and pencil set, and a photograph of a woman whom he assumed was Dr. Endermo's wife, everything was neatly arranged. The rug on the office floor was a thicker, softer, and more plush carpet than those usually found in clinical offices, and he sensed a warm, even feminine touch to the coordination of colors in the soft velvet settee, the thick-cushioned, highback easy chair, the standing lamps and small side tables, and the drapes over the two windows behind Dr. Endermo's desk.

There were the usual plaques and framed degrees on the walls, but there was also a print of a painting Neil recognized to be Asher Durand's *Kindred Spirits*, depicting William Cullen Bryant and his friend, the painter Thomas Cole, standing on a promontory overlooking a rocky brook. Behind them, the mountains loomed hazy and distant. Neil concluded that Dr. Endermo's office was a warm, cozy environment in which to work.

"So," Dr. Endermo said, "what do you think?" He folded his arms across his chest and waited for Neil's reply.

"I don't know." Neil shook his head. "Twelve years old, you say?"

"Yes, twelve years old. About the age of your present students, I think. Am I right?" Neil nodded. "You look terrified," Endermo said with laughter in his eyes.

"You want an honest reaction?"

"Of course."

"I'm torn between an urge to get up and run out of this place and an urge to ask questions and learn more."

"Understandable," Dr. Endermo said. "And since you haven't run out, I'll take that as a hopeful sign. Ask away."

"From what you say, it sounds as if they've always been confined, kept very secret."

Endermo nodded. "I'm sure you can appreciate the reasons. We had no intentions of being labeled 'Frankensteins.' Mostly, we wanted to avoid the kind of media coverage that would only attract curiosity seekers and exposé magazines to our doorsteps. It would be so unfair, and in the long run, so harmful."

"Um . . . in fact, that's where I think I've seen cases like this . . . those magazines." Endermo's eyebrows rose. "Not that I read them, of course," Neil added quickly. "You can't help seeing them on the stands, though."

"Yes, quite grotesque when portrayed that way and absolutely of no scientific value." Dr. Endermo paused. Neil could see that he was still waiting for some kind of concrete reaction on his part.

"It wouldn't be like starting from scratch," Neil said, thinking aloud. "They've had some basic education. I mean, they are capable," he added. Dr. Endermo's response was so slow in coming that

Neil felt the need to talk on and elaborate, but he didn't know what else to say. Endermo leaned forward, clasping his hands on the desk.

"Yes, they have had some education. Dr. Henderson worked some interesting learning experiments with them. Of course, his wasn't a pedagogical motive, but nevertheless . . . they're capable, no question. And Dr. Weber's been doing educational things. There's certainly an appreciable I.Q. difference between them, too. Beta was tested at an I.Q. of 93 and Alpha at 121; not an uncommon phenomenon even for normal twins."

"That's true."

"Now when Dr. Forster mentioned your name to me and gave me your background, I thought you would be perfect for this assignment," Endermo said, sitting back and once again clasping his hands behind his head. Neil saw that because he was such a tall man, so lanky, he had trouble keeping his legs comfortably under the desk. "He considers you his top man in special education, and in a sense, this isn't much different. You deal with disturbed children every day, right? Many of them suffer from birth defects, too," he added quickly.

"Yes, but . . ."

"And there's no problem getting you the leave of absence. You'll double your salary and have what will probably be the most interesting and educational experience of your life. Just think what you will bring back to your classroom when you return."

"Double my salary? Did you say 'double?'"

"This is a very important project, Neil," Endermo said, his eyes narrowing. "There has been a great deal invested here already."

"I don't know what to say. I mean . . ."

"Dive right in, don't prolong the agony of decision. What do you say to seeing them right now?"

"Right now?"

"Why not?" Dr. Endermo asked, holding up his hands.

"Where do they live?"

"Right here in the institute, of course. They have rather comfortable quarters; a small apartment, actually. We wanted them to achieve a certain degree of independence right from the start, to see just how close to normal lives they could lead. There's a kitchen, a living room, and a bedroom. They have a television set, radio, tape deck . . . all the things kids have nowadays. They love watching television," he said, then smiled, obviously recalling some funny situations. "Although they do argue over what to watch. Normal kids do that, too," he added quickly, "and some parents go out and buy them each a television for their rooms. Obviously, we can't do that."

"The problems must be enormous," Neil said, shaking his head. "Just the business of daily life has to be a terrible ordeal. How do they settle arguments?" Neil asked. Dr. Endermo's eyes brightened. Neil sensed he had intended to stimulate his curiosity; that was his bait.

"You'll learn all that we know about them. You'll read Dr. Henderson's reports, Dr. Bender's records, Jessup's materials—everything—before you go to work with them. We have built up quite a file, as you can imagine."

"Has any of this been circulated in the scientific world?"

"Not yet. The lid's still on this thing until we reach certain stages in the project's development, which is where you will come in. We don't want to go out with anything before we're really ready." He paused, and then smiling, added, "Until they're really ready. But don't concern yourself with that," Dr. Endermo said and stood up. Neil thought he stood close to six five. His long legs and arms, along with his narrow face, made him look like a white Watusi. He had thin, narrow facial features, making the bones in his face emphatic. "So, what do you say? One of their walls is a one-way mirror. We have an observation room."

"A fish bowl. We had one in college to observe expert teachers in action."

"We like to refer to it as a laboratory," Dr. Endermo said, softly. Neil detected a slight twinge just before he said it and wondered if it was because Dr. Endermo was sensitive to any implication of cruel experimentation. "Believe me, their comfort and happiness is foremost in our thinking," he added and Neil concluded that Endermo had to be sensitive to such criticism. *It was understandable*, he thought. "Come along and see for yourself," Dr. Endermo said. He walked to the door. Neil hesitated, then stood up. "Good," Dr. Endermo said, putting an arm around his shoulders. "Relax. You're about to see something you'll never forget, something that will change your life forever."

Once again Neil was impressed with the heavy silence in the corridors. As soon as he and Dr. Endermo crossed out of the area that housed the administrative offices and moved farther away from the hospital itself, voices and noise became less and less noticeable until they were gone altogether. Doors to laboratories and offices were closed and identified only by impersonal numbers; there were no windows to the outside along the way. Long fluorescent lights threw a clean, pale-white light over the gray walls.

Now the sound of their own footsteps echoed down the polished floors. Although Neil was six feet tall, he felt considerably shorter as he accompanied the much taller man. Dr. Endermo walked at a steady pace, but his eyes darted about, searching doorways. He seemed to be anticipating something, fearful that someone would pop out and say or do what they shouldn't.

"And I thought the school building was too spread out," Neil said.

"People who work down in this section have their own parking lot. Once you have clearance, you'd have a relatively short distance to go every morning."

"I didn't mean to sound worried about it. I'm one of these modern day fitness freaks," he said, and immediately regretted the use of the word "freaks," but Endermo didn't seem to pick up on it.

"Tell me, Neil," he said without looking at him. "Why do you work with special students?"

"Why?" He thought for a moment. "It's more exciting to make a breakthrough with them."

"Why is that?" Endermo asked.

"Well, for one thing, growth with the so-called normal child is often long in coming and hard to distinguish. The way school systems are set up now, kids move from one teacher to another every year. You just get to know a kid and he moves on; it underlines the great superficiality in our methods. At least, I think so." Neil realized he had broken out into one of his pet lectures, but he had to go on. "I have kids all day in a contained environment. Most of them will spend three or four years with me. I see the changes. When they grasp concepts like plurals, possession, degree—things we take for granted, it's exciting. I feel a sense of real accomplishment."

"Interesting," Endermo said flatly. "Because if you feel that way now," he added, turning to him, "you can just imagine what you'd feel working here."

"Figured that was what you were up to when you asked me," Neil said, nodding. Dr. Endermo laughed.

"I'd better be on the up and up with you, I see. Forster tells me you're a magna cum laude from State University at Albany. Always a scholar, were you?"

"Hardly. I didn't start to take an interest in school until I was in tenth grade."

"What happened in the tenth grade? We have a little ways more to go here," Dr. Endermo added, pointing ahead.

"I had this English teacher, Gene Madeo. Quite a guy. Lighthearted, but deeply sensitive. He didn't hesitate to chuck out the system if it got in the way of real education."

"Inspired you?"

"Yeah, as corny as that sounds."

"It's not corny, not at all."

"Anyway, I saw the possibilities," Neil continued. "The power to affect people, to change and direct their lives."

"You like that kind of power?"

"Well, I didn't mean to make it sound like I like the power. I like making a difference."

"Don't we all," Dr. Endermo said. "Don't we all. And that's the magic in doing this kind of work, Neil. I hope you see that," Dr. Endermo said, his voice filled with that tone of enthusiasm again. Neil nodded. They stopped before a door with no number. It looked more like the door to a closet. "Here we are."

He took out a key from his lab robe pocket and opened the locked door. They entered a small hallway with a door on the immediate left and one directly in front of them. Dr. Endermo went to the front door and unlocked that one, too. They walked into a small, narrow room, with walnut-brown paneling and a beige tile floor. It had a row of folded chairs and two small desks. There was nothing on the desks and nothing on the walls. The light from the apartment came through the one-way window.

"Have a seat," Dr. Endermo said, and Neil followed him to the front row. They stared into the apartment.

It consisted of three small rooms; the kitchen was the smallest. There was a bathroom off the bedroom. The living room had only a few pieces of furniture that looked thrown together randomly—a stiff-looking, antique, white vinyl couch with one table on the right end, a rather large white-and-beige cushioned chair with a lamp beside it, a table in the center, and a television set directly across from the couch; there was a stereo unit against the rear wall. The walls were papered in a green, striped pattern and there was a soft-looking, fluffy, greenish-brown carpet on the floor.

The bedroom simply had a king-size bed and one night table. It was lit by an overhead fixture that threw a sickly yellowish glint over the light-brown walls. There was a greenish-brown carpet in the bedroom, too. The kitchen had a small table and four chairs, one oversized. All the appliances were built into the far wall. The walls were light yellow, and bare—not a picture, not a calendar, nothing.

At first Neil saw no one. Then the bathroom door opened and the twins emerged.

Even with all that Dr. Endermo told him, Neil was not prepared for this. He thought no one could be. He sat forward, almost as if magnetically drawn to what had appeared before him. He wasn't even aware that he was holding his breath.

Both girls had long, well-brushed, light-brown hair resting neatly just below their shoulders. Everything about their facial features seemed normal, and in fact, they had pretty faces: small, button noses; high-boned cheeks; rich, healthy complexions. Neil was aware of Dr. Endermo looking at him and measuring his reaction, but he couldn't help gawking. It was freakish, interesting, and horrifying all at once. There was a part of him that wished to express pity and sadness, but there was a part of him that enjoyed the weirdness of it all.

They were joined at the waist: two complete upper bodies, two arms for each—but then they became two persons sharing two legs. Above the waist they leaned away from each other as much as possible, but they had a common lower stomach and pelvis.

They were dressed in a pair of jeans and two light-blue sweatshirts covered with the emblems of cartoon characters. They wore sneakers with no socks. Alpha, the one on the right, seemed to be carried along by the movement of the walking. From one angle it appeared as if someone was standing directly behind someone else and leaning out.

"Fascinating, aren't they?" Dr. Endermo finally said. There was a look of crazed excitement on his face now; he was more animated than he had been all day. His eyes were wide and his mouth was pulled back in a grotesque smile.

"What do you call what's happened? I mean, is

there a technical term?" Neil found himself speaking in a low volume, nearly a whisper.

"Well, the term 'Siamese twins' is the popular one. Actually it's a misnomer from the famous Chang and Eng in Siam in 1811. Technically, this is *Duplicitas Anterior*."

"How? I mean, why does it happen?"

"The how's easier to answer. Normal identical twins develop when a fertilized ovum splits into two parts, each of which then proceeds to develop into a complete individual. If the splitting is incomplete, however, some degree of linkage—conjoining—occurs in the offspring. When they're of equal size, two symmetrically developed individuals fused together, we call them equal conjoined twins. That's what we have here."

"There must be a hundred questions going through my mind about them."

Dr. Endermo laughed and stood up. He leaned against the one-way window and casually reached over to a dial on the wall. When he turned it, sounds from inside the apartment came through the speakers built into the ceiling of the observation room. The twins had walked over to the television set. One read a television guide while the other played with the channels. Suddenly their voices came over the speakers. Neil's face lit with curiosity and excitement. It was hard to accept that they spoke and sounded the same as other children.

"Don't you want to know what happened to the nurse?"

"I want to watch that quiz show with the cross-word puzzle on the wall."

"But don't you want to know if she's going to live?"

"No."

"But don't you care?"

"No. Why should I care?"

Neil leaned toward Dr. Endermo.

"Which one wants to watch the daytime serial?" he asked.

"Beta."

The quiz show came on and the twins walked back to the couch and sat down. Beta leaned on the arm of the couch in a sulk while Alpha sat straight back, her arm resting over the back of the couch and behind Beta. She had a slight smile of satisfaction on her face. Neil thought there was something attractive, almost angelically innocent about her smile.

"Quite unusual names. Who named them, their parents?"

"No." Endermo looked as though he was smiling himself, although it was hard to tell because his face was turned aside. "Actually, I named them," he finally said.

"Their parents didn't mind?"

"Well, Neil, their parents gave them up immediately after they were born. I'm sure you can understand how they felt."

"Yes," he said. Just before he was going to ask something else, Alpha turned around and looked into the mirror as though she could see him. The look on her face sent a chill down his spine. She seemed to be looking directly into his eyes.

"They can't see us, can they?" he asked quickly.

"Absolutely not," Endermo said. A moment later Alpha turned back to the television set.

"Do they both have control of the movement in their legs?"

"No. Fortunately, they don't. If they did, they probably wouldn't ever coordinate. Beta controls the legs. You'll see the X rays and read all the physiological data that we have on them. Dr. Henderson is in charge of that aspect," Dr. Endermo said.

"So Alpha has to go where Beta wants?"

"Yes. When they were younger, they fought a lot over that. We had a good psychologist working with them: Dr. Mary Jessup. She died a little over a year ago and we replaced her with Dr. Tania Weber. She'll be your consultant and advisor, always available to discuss any problems you might encounter."

"Right now the idea of tutoring them terrifies me. I think I'd end up just gawking at them, like I'm doing now."

"Well, you're not going to go right in there. You'll spend a reasonable orientation period. Believe me, Neil, after a while you won't think of them as terribly unusual."

"That I can't believe."

"Once you've met with some of the other members of the team and see how they react to the twins, you'll understand what I mean. We all achieve a professional level in order to function.

From what I understand about you, you will, too. Weber will explain how important it is that they not be made to feel . . ."

"Freakish?"

"Exactly."

They both turned back to the window as Beta's voice came over the speakers again.

"This is a stupid show. All those letters. It's boring."

"Be quiet."

"If that nurse dies today . . ."

"She won't die."

"She reminds me of Mrs. Cohen."

"Every nurse on television reminds you of Mrs. Cohen."

"Who's Mrs. Cohen?" Neil whispered.

"They had a nurse right up to last year, but as I said, we're trying to get them to be more independent."

"They do have pretty faces," Neil said.

"Why shouldn't they? There's nothing wrong with that part of them." Neil looked up at Endermo and nodded. "If you've seen enough for now, I'll introduce you to Dr. Weber. She's very anxious to meet you."

Neil shook his head slowly.

"Right now it seems too unreal, and I'm looking right at them," he added. "But I have to confess, they are fascinating."

"And when you learn more about this, you'll be even more interested," Endermo said with confidence. He reached for the door handle, but the moment he touched it, he pulled his hand back as if he had touched fire.

"Ouch!" he exclaimed, shaking his hand.

"What is it?"

"Probably just static electricity. My hand feels as if it fell asleep." He opened and closed his fist. "You know the feeling—that tingling in the tips. It's nothing," he added, and opened the door quickly this time, but he continued to open and close his fist. Neil looked down at the floor. There wasn't a rug; he wondered what would have caused such static electricity.

He was drawn to look back into the apartment and saw Alpha looking their way again, this time a definite smile on her face. Neil turned to Dr. Endermo to see if he saw her, too, but he was already out the door. When Neil looked back again, Alpha had turned away.

They walked out to the hall, Dr. Endermo locking all the doors behind them.

"You okay?" he asked. Endermo was still opening and closing his hand.

"What? Oh yeah, sure. Nothing really."

"You're sure they can't see through that mirror?"

"Absolutely." Endermo smiled reassuringly.

"So," Neil said as they continued down the corridor. "You told me how it happened, but not what caused it."

"There's no simple explanation and there's no complete agreement about it," Dr. Endermo said quickly.

"What are some of the theories?"

"Nature goes haywire. There are all sorts of explanations for it. Some right wingers blame it on the Russians," Dr. Endermo said and laughed.

"Are you trying to pinpoint those causes? Is that part of the experimentation here?" Neil asked.

"Oh, certainly," Dr. Endermo said, but there was something in his tone of voice that for the first time made Neil skeptical about his information and gave him a negative vibration. It was only a passing feeling, however, that died an instant death the moment he met Tania Weber.

"Tania," Dr. Endermo said, "this is Neil Richards."

Tania Weber turned from her file cabinet and Neil was pleasantly surprised by what he saw. He had formed a stereotype in his mind, imagining her to be an older woman, clinical, coldly academic because she was part of a research team. Instead, he confronted a soft-faced, green-eyed woman with light, almond-colored skin, who looked to be about twenty-five or twenty-six. She wore her dark-brown hair cut just under her ears and swept up around her cheek bones, framing her face. She was dressed in a matching tweed skirt and jacket. The ruffled collar of her white blouse was up around her neck, almost in a Nehru style.

"Oh, yes. Pleased to meet you," she said, coming away from the cabinet. He shook her extended hand gently, noting the gracefulness of her fingers and wrist. "It's about time they got me a professional educator," she said. She looked to Dr. Endermo with feigned annoyance, then smiled at Neil.

"I'm not sure that's exactly what you need," Neil said. He still held her hand. There was a moment's pause and then he realized it and let go so quickly, it was as if her hand were on fire.

"Oh?" She tilted her head slightly to the right, a gesture he found endearing.

"Neil has just had his first introduction to the twins," Dr. Endermo said.

"Oh, I see," Tania said as if that explained everything.

"Not something that can be forgotten easily," Neil said. He looked at Dr. Endermo, who closed and opened his eyes gently.

"Tania will fill you in and explain your function more fully," Dr. Endermo said. "I'll leave you two alone to discuss things. Got to get back to the office. Stop by when you're finished here, Neil, and we'll talk some more."

"Fine." He watched Endermo leave, then turned as Tania Weber went around to her desk and sat down.

"Sit down, please. Do I call you Neil or Mr. Richards?"

"That depends. Do I call you Dr. Weber or Tania?" he replied. He expected a laugh, but she simply nodded.

"I know what you mean. In places like this, everyone's got one title or another. Just Tania, please."

"Just Neil." He sat down and looked around her office. It was as neat as Endermo's and just as warm and comfortable. There were bright blue curtains on the windows. The walls were painted a light blue and there was a tight knit aqua carpet on the floor.

On the wall to his right, she had a print of a Giacomo Balla painting, *Little Girl Running on a Balcony*. The abstract had been done so as to give a strong feeling of movement, and the dominant turquoise color appeared to coordinate well with the other colors in the office.

As in Dr. Endermo's office, there were the usual plaques and degrees on the wall behind her, but everything was in a soft, wood frame. He saw two letters in frames and imagined they came from superiors, complimenting her on her work. The wall to his left was primarily covered with shelves of books, studies, and texts.

"So, what do you think so far?" she asked.

"Still too shocked to think. How do you get to Dr. Endermo's clinical detachment? I assume you have."

"Oh, it comes eventually. He's an impressive man, I know, but you'll find him refreshingly modest even though he's treated presidents."

"Presidents? Really? For what, birth defects?" Neil started to laugh, but she held her expression.

"No," she said softly. "He's done many other things. You have to understand. This is a special assignment, one of a kind."

"I'll say it's special. Are you serious, he's treated presidents?"

"Tell me about yourself," she said sitting back

and pressing her fingers together. "We can talk about him anytime. I know your teaching experience is with special education students, but how do you feel about the twins? I remember my first view of them," she added quickly. "As surprising as it may sound, it goes away."

"What does?"

"That feeling of being in the presence of double monsters." She smirked after saying it. "That's how they refer to them in textbooks. I'll show you." She got up and went to the shelves to retrieve a book. He studied the way the lines of her hips took shape against her skirt. "It's not my terminology, of course. Believe me, I wouldn't think of referring to them in those terms," she said handing the book to him. "Pages 104 to 111," she said and went back to her desk.

He looked down at the book.

"What drew you into this?" he asked, looking at some of the pictures of other specimens.

"It's like exploring outer space, touching virgin territory. I mean," she said, her voice suddenly taking on a softer, more feminine tone, "there has been quite a bit of work done with twins, good studies of sibling rivalry, personality contrast, and the like, but even though this is something real, it's bigger than reality." She paused, seeing how he was just staring at her. "I don't know if I can make you understand without your having worked with them," she said. She leaned across the desk to open a cigarette box.

"No, thanks."

"Well," she said, sitting back to light her cigarette, "let's begin. Dr. Endermo requires a weekly
report. Occasionally, he calls us all together to
discuss progress. Right now that includes Dr.
Henderson, Dr. Bender, and myself. It was during
one of these sessions that we discussed getting a
tutor."

"Why did you people wait so long to hire a tutor?"

"I can speak only for the last year," she said. "But
apparently there has always been the general belief
that they wouldn't live long. They didn't want to
start them on something and get too many people
involved and then have it end abruptly." She
stopped and looked at him. He waited, expecting
more.

"I don't understand. What changed their minds?
Surely they don't expect them to live normal lives,
do they?"

"I don't know exactly. I . . . well, I really just
began working with them this past year and . . . "

"In other words you don't know the answer
yourself," he said, not realizing he was pursuing her
like a prosecutor. "I guess normal procedures just
wouldn't have made sense with something like
this," he added quickly. "Dr. Endermo told me their
parents gave them up immediately. I didn't ask but
I imagine their parents never saw them again?"

"Most people would rather forget this as soon as
possible."

"Then it's more than likely they don't even know
they're still alive," he said, almost to himself.

"I guess not. I don't know." She blew her smoke straight up toward the ceiling and stared at him.

"Does it bother them that they have no parents?"

She stood up to walk around the desk. Her posture was almost military now. He sensed an effort to subdue what was soft and feminine in order to achieve a neutral demeanor as if revealing her femininity would detract from her professionalism.

"From what I understand, it didn't until they put a television in there. When I first started, I used to get a hundred questions about families, etc."

"So then they fully realize what they are?"

"Oh, of course. They know all the words—freaks, monsters. Look," she said suddenly, revealing a note of impatience he didn't expect. "They're nowhere near normal children. That's why they want a person in special education."

It was obvious that everyone had a delicate sensitivity here, he thought. He wondered if he would develop it, too, should he accept the assignment.

"Tell me about their mental condition. How do they relate to one another?"

"They've gone through major changes in that regard; Jessup's papers are fascinating reading. You should start with that. In the very beginning Beta tormented Alpha a great deal. She realized she had the power of locomotion and used it. Then, that suddenly changed as if she understood her sister's position." She leaned against the desk and laughed. "God, that sounds funny, considering."

He smiled. He was grateful for the light moment.

"This is crazy. I can't do this." He shook his head and put the book she had given him on her desk.

"Sure you can," she said.

"Was there ever a case of equal conjoined twins that went beyond them in years?"

"Chang and Eng."

"Endermo mentioned them, but he didn't give any details."

"They lived to be 63, without being separated; they were joined at the head. They worked for P. T. Barnum, were married, and had eleven children between them." She smiled and shook her head. "There I go again . . . eleven children between them . . . puns just pop up."

"Were the children all right?"

"Yes. Their wives lived in separate houses."

"Incredible." He shook his head.

"When you start this, you'll find out what incredible really means."

He stared at her a moment.

"I've been doing so well with my kids. I hate to leave them for a—"

"Couple of freaks? This isn't some circus act in disguise. Some of the best minds around are part of this project. I'm truly in awe of some of the people who came down these halls."

When she spoke so intently, her eyes got smaller and she took on an intellectual excitement he found stimulating.

"What if one of them gets sick?"

"Well, Dr. Henderson will explain the physiological details. They share a blood supply, of course, so when one gets something, the other usually does." She leaned back to snuff out her cigarette in the ashtray on her desk. "There are things about them we're all just learning," she said.

"Like?"

"I'd rather you formed your own impressions."

He sensed her eagerness to leave the topic and that made him more curious.

"This Mary Jessup . . . what happened to her?"

Tania Weber stared at him a moment, then shook her head as though she were trying to deny the question.

"Endermo said she died," Neil continued.

"Yes. An accident."

"Accident? What kind of accident?"

"Freak accident," she said and then bit down gently on her lower lip. "There I go again with puns."

"You mean it had something to do with the twins?"

"It happened in their apartment, yes. She was having lunch with them and something got caught in her throat. She choked to death right in front of them."

"Oh my God. They didn't know enough to call for help?"

"Well, they probably didn't understand what was happening to her. By the time someone got there . . . she was already blue."

"Shocking, and the effect it must have had on them." He shook his head, but when he looked at her, he didn't detect any sympathy for the twins. "What sort of an effect *did* it have on them?" he asked.

"Very little," she said.

"I don't understand. How can something like that have very little effect?"

"I don't fully understand it yet myself. Whenever I talk about it with them now, it's almost as if it was something that happened on television a long time ago. Neither of them remembers it very vividly, but Beta does more than Alpha."

"Maybe they just repress it. Too painful a memory. Were they close with her?"

"They don't seem to get close with anyone. They have a way of maintaining a detachment."

"They seem to have compassion. When I looked in on them just now with Dr. Endermo, Beta seemed very concerned about something happening to a nurse on a soap opera."

"Yes," she said. "But just as they would forget about the nurse a week after it happened and get hooked on some other program, they seemed to have forgotten about Mary Jessup. I suppose it's all due to their points of moral reference and their sense of reality and illusion. Aside from the people involved in the project, their only contact with the world has been through that television set."

"Maybe it has something to do with their weird physiology," he said.

"Their physiology is not our department," she said. She paused. "And that's the only thing that's a serious no-no here: crossing into someone else's area of expertise." She leaned across her desk and smiled. "Geniuses are very sensitive," she whispered as if the office were bugged.

He stared at her a moment, for he sensed she was deadly serious about this. It was the second time since he began his visit here today that he had a negative vibration, but he didn't pay any more attention to it than he had to the first negative feeling, and for the same reason: Tania Weber's attractive smile.

He vaguely wondered if that wasn't something he would soon regret.

2

"Neil," Dr. Endermo said, extending his hand. "Welcome to what I'm sure is going to be the most exciting teaching experience of your life."

"No doubt about that," Neil said. He had returned to Dr. Endermo's office to tell him he was going to take the assignment. Endermo grimaced when Neil shook his hand.

"Still a little sore from that static electric discharge," he explained, closing and opening his fist.

"Oh? Maybe you should have someone look at it."

"No, it's nothing. So," he said, returning to his desk. "There is only one thing I'll have to emphasize and insist on, and that is that you keep the details of this project to yourself." He sat down and leaned forward on his desk, his hands clasped together with such intensity, the knuckles of his fingers whitened. "I mean, don't even discuss it with your friends at school. When people ask what you're doing up here, tell them you're working with disturbed children at the institute . . . kids with handicaps, both mental and physical, work similar to what you're doing now."

"I see," Neil replied. "You people really mean to keep this top secret."

"It's nothing to worry about," Dr. Endermo said quickly, sensing Neil's discomfort. "As I explained earlier, we must avoid publicity, any publicity. Up until now, we've done well in that respect. You can just imagine what publicity could do to the twins," he added, sitting back, his shoulders relaxing.

"Just who *does* know about this?"

"Basically, only the team. I report to my superiors, of course, but other than that . . . "

"Who are your superiors? I don't recall your mentioning them earlier."

"The institute is a private corporation, Neil, but we get government financing, grants, etc. So, when I say 'my superiors,' unfortunately, I also mean a number of bureaucrats. Being in education, you can appreciate what that means," he added and smirked.

"What about my superintendent, Dr. Forster? He's the one who sent me over here. You had to tell him, right?"

"Forster knows we're dealing with Siamese twins, but he has no idea about the details," Endermo said.

"Details?"

"I left him with the impression the twins were separated," Endermo said, his voice dropping. To Neil it sounded like a confession of guilt.

"But surely you can trust a man like Dr. Forster."

"No question about it. Of course I trust him, but why should I burden him with the responsibility of keeping our little secret, eh? Then he has to worry about accidentally saying something. You understand, I'm sure."

"Yes," Neil said softly.

"I think for the exact same reasons, you should keep the specific details from your parents, too."

"My parents?"

"Neil, people on the outside who are not privy to the details and the possibilities of what we are doing here will just not appreciate it. Even your parents might be upset. They just wouldn't understand and then, if they should say something accidentally . . . well, why put them through it?"

Neil nodded.

"I guess I'll just tell them what Dr. Forster knows."

"Sure. Then there will be no problems. Well then," Dr. Endermo said, standing and coming around his desk. "Once again, welcome to the team, Neil."

"Thanks—I think."

"Oh, you'll enjoy this, you'll see. Now, your school year ends next week. Are you planning a vacation?"

"No. I'll be around except for an overnight visit home."

"Good. Then we can start you on salary say, the first of July?"

"Fine." Neil stood up. "Maybe I can take home some of the reports to read in the meantime."

"No," Dr. Endermo said sharply, so sharply that he was instantly embarrassed by his reaction himself. "I mean, we never let information like that out of the clinic. You'll have all the time you need to prepare, but you'll have to do it in here. Again," he said in a much softer tone of voice, "we have the problem of someone else possibly reading it and talking about it and . . . " He shook his head. "I'm sorry about all this secrecy stuff." He shook his head. "Hate it myself, but I'd hate to see anything ugly happen to those girls."

"I understand," Neil said and went to the door. "The first of July then," he added and left.

He paused outside Dr. Endermo's office and gazed up the corridor in the direction of the twins' apartment. Suddenly Alpha's face materialized before him, wearing the same expression she had when she had turned toward him in the observation room, but the image reappeared so vividly and so intently that it seemed like more than a recollection. He thought he was actually seeing her before him once again. Her eyes were so cold, her gaze so mesmerizing, he couldn't move a muscle. It was as if he were back in that room gaping through the observation window. He felt a great desire to do so and began to take a few steps toward their apartment, walking slowly and then faster. He was about to run down the corridor when he felt a hand on his shoulder.

Alpha's face popped out of his mind as if it had been mounted on a bubble and the bubble had burst. He spun around and faced Dr. Endermo.

"Neil," he said smiling. "Don't tell me you're lost already. Usually takes a day or so."

"I . . . " Neil looked back down the corridor toward the twins' apartment and then at Dr. Endermo. He was confused himself as to why he was where he was. "Yeah, I guess, I wasn't thinking and just started in the wrong direction."

"No problem. You remember how to get out now?"

"Yes. I feel like a jerk. It's not that hard. Thanks," he said. "See you on the first," he added and started away quickly, feeling a little embarrassed. When he looked back, Dr. Endermo was still watching him. The man waved and Neil waved back and went out to the parking lot.

Something happened as he walked toward his car. The farther he got from the building, the better he felt. It was as if he had been a patient, confined to a room and a bed, frustrated by illness, and had just now been released to go home. While he was in there, he felt as though he were trapped under glass like the twins. The memory of Alpha's face was still vivid. She made him sense the frustration she and her sister must feel.

It gave him a chill. He shuddered and stopped to take a deep breath before continuing. Then he quickly started for his car again, not looking back at the building. He couldn't help feeling a little intimidated by the massive structure. The research center was a long stone building that ran off the hospital wing like an afterthought. Contrasted to the lively and busy hospital building on the other side, the "compound" appeared gloomy and ominous to him. It was, after all, surrounded by a high wire fence and had a security guard at the gate.

After he got into his car and drove out, he glanced in his rearview mirror to look back at the front entrance. Housed within were two strange creatures, freaks of nature under a microscope. To be part of all that now seemed repulsive, even though both Dr. Endermo and Tania Weber made him feel it was an exciting experiment. He expected he would back out after he had returned to his apartment and had given it more thought.

But then as he drove down the long entrance road, he considered some of the things Tania Weber had said. He could certainly understand the scientific value to it all and even the educational value. She was right; he would probably come out of it a much wiser, finer teacher. And there was that attractive salary.

He realized that once he had started, he would have to go through with it anyway. The school would get a temporary replacement for him and he wouldn't be able to get his job back until the year ended. Since it was a leave without pay from the school, he would have to find another way to earn a living. So in effect, he would have to stick with this once he committed.

Right after college, he had returned to the Catskills of upstate New York to teach in the Centerville school district because he wanted to avoid the big districts, ones that had teaching staffs as large as the entire high school population of his hometown school. He had been raised in a small, rural community fifty miles northwest of Centerville. His parents still lived there, and they were happy he had begun working in a school system relatively close by. He could drop in to visit at will, and help fill the emptiness that had come into the family since his older brother Brody, a marine, was killed along with more than 200 others in Lebanon during the infamous terrorist attack there.

His mother, now a small, sixty-year-old woman, made even smaller by family tragedy, always saw something happy and something sad in his visits. He and Brody had been so close that they were often interchangeable in their parents' minds. *How many times since Brody's death has Mom called me Brody?* he thought. *Talk about Siamese twins.*

His father was a retired postal worker, a conservative, Reagan Republican who had had his faith shaken. Normally outspoken and eager to get into political debates, he had become somewhat withdrawn since Brody's death. Neil and his father used to have some lively arguments about politics, but now, there was an unspoken truce. Both were afraid to bring up any topic that might lead them back to the situation causing Brody's death.

He couldn't help but wonder what their reaction to his taking this assignment would be if he told them the whole truth. He was sure Dr. Endermo didn't want them to know simply because they might talk him out of it. Of course they knew about the Mandicott Clinic; everyone within a hundred mile or so radius did. It was rapidly becoming one of the state's finest and most respected hospitals. The planners had been aesthetically minded, too, to have it constructed in a beautiful, rural setting, nestled in a small valley. It served a continually growing population of families whose breadwinners were New York commuters.

But few knew what other things went on within its walls. Now he was one of them. Could he go ahead with it? *Why not?* he thought. If a woman as intelligent and as attractive as Tania Weber could . . . He couldn't help thinking about her. In fact, she was so heavy in his thoughts that he was almost not surprised to hear from her a little over an hour after he had left the research institute. Perhaps he had conjured her up the same way he had conjured up Alpha's face.

At first he thought she was calling because she and Dr. Endermo had sensed he wasn't really sold on taking the position and they were going to do some more lobbying, but that wasn't her reason.

"Dr. Endermo tells me you're starting on the first of July," she said.

"Yes. Do you take a vacation during the summer?"

"Two weeks in August, but it's adjustable," she said quickly. "The reason I called you though was to ask if Dr. Endermo had actually introduced you to the twins. I remember your telling me you observed them, but . . ."

"Introduced? No. In fact, he told me I should

spend a period of time observing them before actually facing them."

"Yes, I thought that would be the procedure." Her voice drifted and he sensed her deep thought.

"So . . . what made you ask?"

She was silent for a long moment.

"Well, I went in to see the twins and Alpha acted as if they had already met you."

"She did?" For some reason, just hearing that started his heart thumping. "She looked at me when we were in the observation room, but Dr. Endermo assured me she couldn't see through the mirror."

"No, she can't."

"Well, I don't understand. Why did you say she acted as if they had met me?"

"I told them about you. Beta acted very excited about it, but Alpha acted as if she knew all about it. It's nothing," she said after a moment. "Probably her usual emotional control. When I explained to them that it would be a while yet, Beta was very disappointed."

"It's still a frightening prospect to me," Neil said. He wondered if he should describe his strange visual experience in the corridor, but he didn't want to sound like some kind of a nut. It had to have been his imagination anyway, a result of all the shocking things he had seen and learned.

"Relax. You're going to enjoy this. Looking forward," she said and hung up before he could ask her any more questions.

Suddenly he wished he hadn't made such an

impulsive decision to take the job. It was so unlike him anyway to decide something without going over and over it. Why, it took him hours to chose the clothes to buy. Usually, he treated each and every decision as though it were of major significance. Some of his friends kidded him about it, telling him to begin his Christmas shopping in January.

What had made him decide to do this so quickly, he wondered, especially a decision that really was of major significance to his life? Now that he thought back to his meetings with Dr. Endermo and Tania Weber, he couldn't explain it himself. While he was in there, it had come over him. He had suddenly felt he wanted to do it; he had to do it.

His decision to take the leave of absence stimulated a great deal of chatter in the faculty room at school the next day. Naturally, his fellow teachers bombarded him with questions. He found himself fabricating facts and information to cover up what he was actually going to do. Only Mac Denin, a history teacher for nearly thirty years, pursued him for more details.

Mac was the recognized dean of the staff, occasionally even called upon to substitute for the principal. Younger, more inexperienced teachers usually gravitated toward him, drawn to him magnetically because of his wisdom and seasoning. He had been sitting back quietly listening to Neil's responses, but soon Mac's two graying, bushy eyebrows began to lift and turn into one another, a sure sign of skepticism and curiosity.

"These kids you'll be working with," he asked, "are in the research division, supervised by members of the research staff?" Everyone knew there was a research center at Mandicott, but no one knew specifically what was going on. There were the usual explanations—medical research, chemical research, even research in prosthetics.

"Apparently. I don't know that much about their setup, Mac." He smiled weakly at the others.

"Well, you said you're working at the compound, right?" he asked, pursuing the point.

"Somewhere in there. I don't have a definite room yet."

"How many kids?"

"Not more than six."

"I wonder who's funding the project," Mac said, thinking aloud. "Do they characterize it as experimental?"

"I really don't know. Never asked." He shrugged. "The money's great; that's all I know," he added and everyone else laughed. Mac stared at him and nodded slowly.

"Miss you around here, kid," he said.

"Oh, I'll stop by and commiserate with everyone from time to time."

There was more laughter and the tension passed, but it left a bitter taste in his mouth to be untruthful with people he respected, even though the deceit was admittedly for a good cause.

That afternoon, he went into the school library, and using the Reader's Guide, found an article about Siamese twins. He stared at the pictures, then read the copy beneath them.

"Conjoined or Siamese twins occur only about once in every 50,000 or 60,000 births; only about 300 such conjoined children have ever lived more than a few days."

There was a picture of a pair after they had been separated by surgery. The article went on to discuss what doctors would do to make it possible for each of them to live an independent existence.

Only 300 lived more than a few days, he thought, *and these twins had already lived twelve years conjoined*. The sight of two upper bodies emanating from one lower trunk passed before him vividly and again he conjured up Alpha's face. What was that look in her eyes? It was as if she had been studying him, observing him, instead of vice versa. He shook off the image and looked at the reference material again.

I guess, he thought, *what they had accomplished at Mandicott was a remarkable phenomenon*. There was good reason for the secrecy and the excitement, and he was going to be part of it. In time, when the people running the project felt ready, they would reveal it all and he would be part of the team that faced the press. He saw himself on the stage, Alpha and Beta beside him, as he fielded questions about their education. He would be part of an historic project, he concluded. Won't Mac and the rest of them be impressed.

He was overwhelmed with a desire to start

immediately, and he called Dr. Endermo to tell him of his decision.

"That's wonderful, Neil. I'm glad you've got such enthusiasm already. Sure, we'd love to get some of the preliminary work out of the way. In fact, come up here and have a session with Dr. Henderson. He'll fill you in on all you have to know about them physically."

"Fine," he said, and the next day made his appointment to visit with Dr. Henderson, the doctor assigned to the twins' physical health. He suddenly realized that never in his life had he ever pursued something with such intensity. Ever since he had seen the twins, he had thought about them. Not a quiet moment passed without his envisioning them, and every night since he had been there, they were in his dreams.

He was beginning to feel possessed.

Henderson's office was in the basement corridor and at the east end of the research center. The area was a good distance from Dr. Endermo's office, Tania Weber's office, and the twins' quarters. As Neil walked through the dark corridor, lit by an occasional, long fluorescent bulb that made the walls and floors in the illuminated area seem like glass, he wondered why Henderson had been deliberately housed away from everyone else. There was another security guard at the opening to this area. The uniformed man sat at a small table reading a magazine. He seemed grateful for Neil's appearance, for it gave him something to do—check his identification.

Dr. Henderson's office was about a third of the way down the corridor. The area past his office was even darker. Neil saw a nurse go from one room to another, her footsteps echoing like short taps of a small hammer against the dull, brown tile corridor floor, but other than that, he thought there was an ominous silence down here. There was a very unpleasant odor and, despite the warm weather outside, he felt somewhat chilled.

He found Dr. Henderson at his desk in a small, outer office next to the examination room. Even though Neil knew Dr. Endermo had called to tell him Neil was arriving, Dr. Henderson wore an expression of surprise when Neil entered. Neil introduced himself and then, after an initial glance and nod, Dr. Henderson went back to writing something in a folder. Neil waited awkwardly just inside the door.

"Sorry," Henderson said, putting his pen down. "I had something I just had to write down before I forgot it. So you're the teacher," he said, standing up and coming to him. "How do you do?" He thrust his long, slim fingers at Neil in a sharp, jerky motion and shook Neil's hand quickly. He looked distracted, uncomfortable. Neil assumed the man was just naturally shy.

"You're like in the dungeon here," Neil said, hoping to create a relaxed atmosphere quickly. "I kept expecting to hear the sounds of chains and men moaning under torture."

"Oh?" Henderson did not smile.

"Well, you're so far from all the other activities."

"I enjoy having the privacy. So . . ." He stared at Neil for a moment. "You want to learn all about our special twins, eh?"

"As much as I need to know, I guess."

"Right. I don't see the point in my getting very technical here, and I don't see where the technical information will be of any help to you in your function anyhow," he added.

Dr. Henderson was a thin man, standing no more than five feet, ten inches tall. Neil estimated him to be in his mid-forties; he had only a tinge of gray in his dark brown hair. His eyes, the faded brown of bleached beach sand and somewhat magnified by his thick, clear-plastic-frame glasses, moved over Neil intensely. Neil felt himself being evaluated, almost as if he were being auditioned for manual labor.

"Fine with me," Neil said. "I don't want to get in over my head anyway." He looked about Henderson's office nervously. There were charts pinned on the walls, a large IBM clock above his cluttered desk, a scale in the right corner, and a wall light for X rays on the left. The walls of the offices in this section of the institute were simply plastered sheet rock and the floors were hard tile. He noted there was no window in Henderson's office.

"Sensible," Henderson said. "That's when most people get into trouble—when they try to do things beyond their capabilities. So . . . let's see, where shall we start?"

He didn't look at Neil when he spoke to him. Instead, he turned back to the desk and flipped through pages of reports and small folders.

"I can't help but have a natural curiosity about the body they share," Neil said, following it with a short, nervous laugh.

Henderson nodded, then walked over to the X rays he had hanging on the wall. He flipped a switch on the side and the films lit up. Neil stepped closer. Henderson waited, expecting him to approach. He didn't look back. He just began.

"As you can see here, they have special spinal columns joined with a common pelvis. They share the same large intestine, and arteries in their bodies are connected. In other words," he said pedantically, "their blood supply is pumped throughout both their upper bodies."

"Why is it that only one controls the legs?"

"Only one has a fully developed sciatic nerve."

"Don't you find that extraordinary?" Neil asked.

Henderson turned around and looked at him as if Neil had said the most outrageous thing. He peered up over his glasses at him in silence for a long moment.

"Why?"

"It's as if Nature knew they couldn't get along any other way," Neil said and smiled.

Henderson flipped off the light without responding, then walked back to his desk.

"I don't know. It just seemed amazing to me," Neil said to fill the heavy pause.

"Nature, as you call it, simply screwed up here

altogether," Henderson said. "I don't find any of this amazing. On the contrary, I find it distorted."

"Well, I just meant . . ."

"Don't expect that they'll both tire at the same time or they'll both have interests at the same time," Dr. Henderson said, obviously impatient with the topic. "They have two brains and the brain is the most complicated part of the body. It controls a great deal more than a layman would expect," he said pronouncing "layman" as if it were a profanity.

Neil nodded and looked back at the X rays even though the light was off and he could barely make anything out.

"How old were they here?"

"Six years, four months."

"I see it," Neil said shaking his head, "but I still can't believe it. Dr. Endermo explained how it happened, but he didn't have any answers concerning the why."

Henderson turned and stared at him for a moment.

"Well, there are many possible causes for birth defects, Mr. Richards. Some are environmental, some are drug related. And some are mysterious . . . something goes haywire in the genes."

"Do we know what caused them to be the way they are?"

"No," Henderson said. "That wasn't our concern at the time. The research being done here involves human relationships." He smiled, but Neil felt it was a contrived smile. *The man's a stereotyped research scientist*, he thought. "So, when we had the opportunity for such a detailed study, we grabbed it."

"Do you expect them to live normal life spans now?" Neil asked.

"We didn't expect them to live this long. When one dies, the other dies. We don't have much to go on. Every day there is a new discovery, if you know what I mean."

"Sure."

"Right now, they appear to be in perfect health, although changes in their bodies could happen overnight."

"Should I watch for anything?"

"No," Henderson said, smiling more sincerely. Apparently he found the suggestion genuinely amusing. "They are checked on a daily basis. They have twenty-twenty vision, excellent hearing, no speech difficulties. Matter of fact, you should have a relatively easy time of it, considering what you have been working with up until now."

"What?" Neil started to laugh, but stopped. He saw Dr. Henderson was serious. He looked back at the X rays and shook his head.

"Why don't you just start your work and when you run into problems that involve me, I'll come into it," Dr. Henderson added, his tone almost friendly.

"Okay, thanks. I've got to get up to Dr. Weber's office and catch up on my reading."

"Fine."

"Thanks again for your time."

"No problem. Good luck with your end," he said and turned back to his papers.

Neil left and closed the door behind him. Just as he turned to go up the corridor, he heard footsteps and looked back to see that nurse he had seen before open a door. He thought he heard the sound of babies crying, but the door was opened and closed so fast, he couldn't be sure.

He waited a moment, then started walking quickly, anxious to leave this section of the institute. He realized their need for isolation, but he couldn't imagine himself working down here. The place gave him the creeps. When he walked upstairs, the long, quiet corridor that led to Tania Weber's office and the twins' apartment was a welcomed change. He felt as if he could breathe again.

"They haven't set up your office yet," Tania told him when he entered her office. "They didn't expect you to start ahead of schedule, so I set up a place for you in here." She had a chair and a table pushed over to the left with a lamp set up on it. There was a typewriter on the table and a small pile of folders beside it. "Hope you'll be comfortable."

"Looks fine."

"How was your meeting with Dr. Henderson?" she asked and pressed her lips together softly as she closed and opened her eyes. The gesture suggested that she anticipated unhappiness.

"Well . . . I learned some new things, but . . ."

"But?"

"I don't know. Henderson gave me the feeling the

whole meeting was unnecessary. Talk about your typical scientist . . . he's the man with microscope eyes."

She laughed, a short, warm laugh that wound itself around him like the scent of her perfume.

"Aptly put. He doesn't have what you might call a doctor's bedside manner. You'll have to forgive him for his failed social graces. He detests small talk. Actually," she said, lowering her voice into a whisper for the dramatics, "he doesn't get along with people directly. He's better at talking to them through X rays, blood tests, even urine samples." Neil laughed. "But he's a recognized genius in his field," she added. "You'll get used to him, at least enough to tolerate him, but you'll never get to know him. He's too involved with his work to care about anything else."

"He strikes me as the type voted most likely to blow the world up," he said.

"Don't worry about him. He won't bother you and you won't have to go see him in his office much."

"Good. That corridor is more like a morgue."

"Exactly. I don't like going there and I really don't. They have all these specimens in bottles. The place reeks of embalming fluid."

"Right," he realized. "That was the terrible odor."

She went to his table. "These are Dr. Jessup's early reports," she said, indicating the folders. "I think you'll find them fascinating. I did."

"Thanks." He moved past her to the chair, but as he did so, their eyes met and he sensed a glint of interest. She seemed to regret it, however, and quickly turned to go back to her own desk. He opened a file.

"Hey," he said, "this is written in the form of a diary."

"I know. She had a style. More than I have, that's for sure. My reports read like lab manuals."

Neil started to read. He quickly lost track of time and place.

February Beta took a few steps today and Alpha was terrified by it. She seems to feel the anxiety coming from uncertainty and the fact that she has no control over where she is carried and whether Beta falls or not. Miraculously, she braces for each flop the way Beta does.

Beta enjoys her newfound power as much as any normal child would. It has taken her longer to attain it because of the extra load (Alpha). Dr. Henderson is confident she will walk as well as any child. He assures me her body will compensate and adjust. As I observe her, I see that she is indeed learning how to handle balance.

The nurse tells me Alpha insists on having her bottle when Beta has hers. If each doesn't have her own, they fight over it. One asset for Alpha—she doesn't seem to be bothered by wet diapers and sleeps better during the night because of that. They nap at different times, although there is no general pattern.

Some confusion as to why they're getting hungry at different times. First theory was that low blood sugar would be experienced simultaneously and cause simultaneous hunger, but they are waking at different times for feeding.

March Significant changes: Beta is gradually taking on the role of caretaker. She knows that Alpha can't get to where she wants or reach what she wants when she wants. Consequently, she either anticipates Alpha's desires or understands them and fulfills them. It is quite interesting. She never takes a cookie without giving one to Alpha first. At times, I get the impression Beta is Alpha's servant. It's almost as if Beta is merely an extension of Alpha.

They are sharing toys now. Oddly enough, whenever there aren't two of something, they ignore it, almost as if they sense they would have a conflict.

Beta's attention span is much shorter, but she is permitting Alpha to influence her interests. There is a whole world of compromise falling into place. Alpha learns a lot faster and grasps concepts quicker. She has better motor control and better visual perception. I know she could go much faster than she does, and I am convinced she is holding herself back to permit Beta to stay with her.

It's uncanny, but right now they seem to lack

any competitive motivation. I don't see the expected sibling rivalry at this age level.

April Beta had an interesting tantrum today. She insisted on placing blocks in the wrong spaces, the same spaces Alpha had placed them in. I refused to let her do it, but I got nowhere until Alpha made the corrections on her materials. There is obviously a great self-identification image between the two. I'm beginning to feel as though they think of themselves as one. I don't know what problems this will cause as they progress, but right now it is obviously hurting Beta more than Alpha.

May Alpha developed whooping cough. Although Beta hasn't gotten it yet, she's coughing. Dr. Endermo agrees with the probability of sympathetic pain, but doesn't go along with my theory concerning the lack of self-image as individuals.

I go back to an earlier idea. Very simply put, I am convinced now that they don't see themselves as separate people. The physical conjoining has caused them to feel that each is an extension of the other. Just as an arm or a leg is a part of an individual, so do they think of one another. It's something I sense Alpha feels the most.

I am directing my efforts now toward getting them to think of each other as a separate person, to be respected and loved as an individual.

As soon as Neil put the folder down, Tania looked up from her desk. He sat there for a moment, staring at nothing. She saw the look on his face and came around to his table.

"Well?"

"It's fascinating, all right. Of course, I have a lot to read yet, but do you feel what Jessup felt about the way they view one another?"

"You mean that idea about each seeing the other as just another appendage?" He nodded. "I did when I first started, but I think they are changing as they grow older and each develops more of a personality. However, there are times when they are so much in sync, it's eerie."

Neil thought for a moment, then nodded.

"I'd better read on," he said and continued to go through the folders. Tania left and returned to the office twice. After the second time, she mentioned she was going to the hospital cafeteria for lunch and he jumped at the opportunity to accompany her.

"What do we do," he joked, "call a cab to get there?"

"I know a short cut," she said, and she did.

They went down to the basement, but instead of turning left toward Henderson's area, they turned right and followed the lower corridor past storage rooms and pipes that brought them to another stairway up into the hospital wing and the cafeteria.

"This place is like some kind of maze," he said. "Or more like the catacombs."

"It's a very big complex and these basement corridors connect and run everywhere," she told him.

The cafeteria was filled with nurse's aides, nurses, and interns, some on lunch hour, some waiting to go on their shift. There was a subdued murmur of conversation in the place, what Neil liked to think of as "hospital silence."

"Where are you from?" he asked Tania after they were seated. They had found a small table that afforded them the most privacy possible in the cafeteria.

"Manhattan would have to be my point of origin, but I've spent years traveling. My father was in the diplomatic corps. He's retired now and lives in North Carolina, practically right on top of a golf course. My mother thinks his love of golf is outright adulterous."

Neil laughed.

"You're from a small town nearby . . . something called Long Eddy?"

"Yes. My family used to spend a good part of the summer up in this area, then eventually settled here."

"Uh huh."

"Where do you live now?" he asked.

"Centerville. The Terrace Apartments."

"No wedding ring, I see," he said, nodding toward her fingers.

"Unattached. One broken engagement with all

the scars. You know the type—not visible, but under the skin, where they really get to you, rest the sharp memories."

"What happened?"

"Luckily, I found out he was already married."

"What?"

"To his work," she said, smiling.

"Oh. I didn't mean to get so personal," he said.

"That's all right. I know a lot about your personal life."

"I had that feeling."

"You're what I call 'Straight Arrow.' A good high school student, president of your senior class, varsity sports, worked on the newspaper, member of Future Teachers of America. There really was such a club?" He nodded, a half smile on his face. "Let's see, what else? No history of drugs, pot, booze. Made Eagle Scout and received a commendation from the president. No distractions or digressions from your career objectives. And," she added smiling, "a registered Republican."

"Just to please my father."

"You drive a Ford," she continued as if delivering a memorized speech from a play, "live in an upgraded apartment complex, and still wear a tie and jacket to work. You went right to work out of college and then got your masters degree, already ran for faculty president and got elected. You've seen a few women on and off this past year, but as of yet, nothing serious."

"Jesus. Am I really that boring?"

She laughed, shrugged, and continued to eat her sandwich. He thought a moment.

"I'm curious. How did you get all that information?"

"Dr. Endermo gave me your folder when he was considering you for the position."

"But why did they do such a thorough background check? I know they would be concerned about my teaching credentials, but the rest of this . . . this isn't a job involving national security."

"No, but it does involve some covert activity. Secrets have to be kept; people have to be trusted. Don't feel bad," she said, "they did the same background check on me. You'd be surprised at the dossier available on the average person in this country. Dr. Endermo has important connections. When he wants to know about someone, he pushes a button and out comes the information."

"Makes you feel like Big Brother has arrived," Neil said. "Can't say I like it," he added, and looked away.

"I know what you mean. Privacy has become a very precious commodity in our society. Sometimes, I feel sorry for the twins because they're under glass twenty-four hours a day."

He stared at her a moment.

"I can't figure you out. You seem out of place here."

"Why?" She followed her question with a short, nervous laugh.

"You're a normal human being, for one thing. You don't walk around with microscopes in your eyes.

Guys like Henderson make my skin crawl. He probably never looks at anyone without thinking— hmm, yes, eyes bulging, overactive thyroid; fiery complexion, high blood pressure."

She laughed at his imitation of a mad scientist.

"I know what you mean, but I'm afraid I do that, too. I'm always analyzing people."

"Really? Well, you're not as obvious about it. I suppose you've been analyzing me, huh?"

"Maybe."

"When do I get the results?"

"I have to run a few more tests yet," she said coyly. He laughed.

"Any chance of one of those tests being run outside of this place?"

She didn't respond for a moment. In fact, he thought she wasn't going to. Then, looking down and playing with the silverware as she spoke, she responded.

"I think, for the time being, we should keep our relationship as professional as possible. It'll be better for your work and mine if we remain somewhat objective about one another."

"I see. Work first and foremost, eh?"

"For a while anyway." She looked up at him. "I'm sorry. I don't mean to sound snobby or anything. It's just that right now, I don't want any distractions."

"Sure. I understand. But that doesn't mean I'm going to stop trying," he said. She laughed and for a moment slipped out of her hard posture. It was long enough for him to instinctively decide she was interesting and worth an investment of time and energy.

Afterward, they returned to her office where he sat and completed his reading of the Jessup files. She left to visit the twins while he was doing so. When she returned, she looked quite flushed. He saw her eyes were bloodshot and realized she had been crying.

"What is it?" he asked. She shook her head and went quickly to her seat behind her desk. He turned around completely and waited for her to get her composure.

"It's Mrs. Gerhart," she said.

"Mrs. Gerhart?"

"The twins' cook."

"What about her?"

"She just—just got electrocuted to death."

"What? How?"

"They're not sure. They think there was some sort of a short in the electric stove in her kitchen and when she touched it . . . a circuit breaker went off, but by the time the custodian traced the problem to her kitchen and found her . . ." She shook her head. "He said there was smoke coming out of her ears."

"My God!"

"That poor woman. She was a widow, supporting herself. She's been with the twins ever since . . . ever since they were brought here. I'm sorry. This is a helluva way to start your first day here."

"What about the twins? Hadn't they heard or seen the accident? Why didn't they call for help?"

"They were in the living room," she said. "The electricity is on a different circuit breaker there. They were watching television." She stared at him a moment, then added, "As if nothing unusual had happened."

3

They were dressed in a blue denim skirt and short-sleeved, white cotton blouses. Their light-brown hair was trimmed neatly just below their ears. Whoever trimmed it took great care to keep both looking precisely the same. Beta wore a plastic hospital identification bracelet on her left wrist, with the letters B E T A embossed. Alpha wore a replica on her right wrist with A L P H A embossed.

When Neil entered just behind Tania, they were sitting in the center of the couch. Beta had her hands clasped and resting on her left leg. Alpha had her hands clasped in a similar fashion and resting against her chest. Both were as curious as kittens, gazing from him to Tania, then centering intently on him.

As he walked through the door, he kept her words of advice in mind: "Be businesslike and keep thinking about the work you are going to do. They'll be watching your reactions very closely, but remember, more than anything, they want to feel comfortable with you."

But would he ever feel comfortable with them? He knew enough about kids, especially handicapped ones, to know that they were extremely sensitive to the way adults reacted to them. In some ways it was harder to lie to children. It was just as he had told Dr. Endermo: he couldn't be sure himself whether or not he would end up simply gawking at them, and he was afraid that would make them so uncomfortable, he would be ineffective.

But he was influenced by Tania's professionalism. He found himself successfully working up the right attitude on entry. He told himself this was just another special classroom and these were just another type of handicapped children.

"Well, girls, here he is, just as I promised," Tania began. "Mr. Richards."

"Hello," Neil said. He flashed a warm smile to hide his nervousness. Beta's face softened and her eyes brightened, but Alpha continued to study him intently, only a slight easing of the muscles around her eyes revealing any relaxation.

"Hi," Beta said.

"Put your materials on the table here, Neil," Tania said, indicating the table in front of the couch, "and we'll all go over them with you."

"Sure," he said. Although he had observed the twins almost a half dozen times since the first day, he looked around as though this were the first time he had seen the apartment. "Very nice in here," he said. He looked at the twins. "Nicer than my classroom back at school," he added and smiled again. Beta looked amazed and interested by the remark, but Alpha smirked. Then, as if she knew something, she turned and looked at the mirror. He felt the heat come into his neck and quickly followed Tania's lead. She sat on their left on the couch and he sat on their right and placed his materials on the table.

He glanced at the mirror himself, catching sight of the reflection of the four of them seated there. From this perspective, it was impossible to see where the twins were conjoined so there was the illusion that he and Tania were sitting with two complete individuals.

For a moment he wondered if Dr. Endermo or anyone else was behind the mirror observing. How often when he was in here would they be? It hadn't struck him until he had entered the "fish bowl" and now the idea disturbed him. He was reminded of the times when he was a probationary teacher and his supervisor would periodically appear to evaluate his teaching. Yet he wasn't concerned so much about whether or not Dr. Endermo and his colleagues thought he was a good teacher. They wouldn't have hired him for such an assignment if they had had any doubts. What concerned him was the way he felt violated under the eye of a Big Brother or under the microscopic eyes of someone like Dr. Henderson.

If he felt this way, he could just imagine what it would be like for the twins should they learn they had been under constant observation and study from the day they were born.

This close to them, he couldn't help but note how perfectly identical they were physically. It was as though a mirror were being held up to one or the other. However, even within this short period of time, he sensed some personality differences. Beta evinced a normal twelve-year-old's excitement and curiosity about her new teacher; Alpha looked skeptical, suspicious, almost angry.

She picked up the top book as soon as he placed them on the table and opened the cover quickly.

"Let me see, too," Beta whined.

"This is going to be hard," Alpha predicted, flipping through the pages. "It's not just arithmetic."

She turned to him sharply to have her statement confirmed. For a moment her cold, hard glare turned his back into jelly. He felt himself sinking into the couch. Beta leaned forward, very interested in his response. Looking at the two of them so closely, he couldn't help but drop his eyes to where they were conjoined. The gesture, as short in duration as it was, seemed to confirm something in Alpha's mind. She bit her lower lip and nodded slightly to herself.

Neil straightened up quickly.

"Nothing will be easy," he said. "But," he added, "with my help, nothing will be really hard either."

"You're a teacher who teaches in a classroom?" Alpha asked.

"That's right."

"This is going to be your classroom now?"

He looked at Tania, who smiled and nodded.

"Yes, it is."

"Then will you bring the others in here to learn?" she demanded.

"I don't want the others," Beta cried. "We don't need them."

"Shut up," Alpha snapped and turned back to him.

"Others?" Neil, half-smiling, looked to Tania again. She shook her head.

"Others like us," Alpha said.

"I told you, Alpha," Tania said in a deliberately tired voice, "there are no others like you. We've been through this so many times," she said, more for Neil's benefit than for theirs. "That's why you live here—because you and Beta are so special."

Alpha turned back to Neil to see if he would confirm what Tania said. Something in his face convinced her he would. Her expression revealed her disappointment.

Neil pulled a workbook out from under the pile of texts.

"You can see that this workbook goes with that textbook," he said quickly. He hoped to ease the tension by doing what Tania had suggested— getting right to business.

"Are there two?" Beta asked.

"Oh yes. There's two of everything."

"Not everything," Alpha said. The point of her innuendo was quite clear. Neil chose to ignore it.

"And this will be your reading text," Neil said. "There are quite a few good stories in it."

"About children?" Beta asked.

"None like us," Alpha interjected, then she looked up to see if Neil would contradict her.

He wiped his forehead with the back of his hand and wondered if he appeared as flushed as he felt. Tania cleared her throat to indicate he should stay on target and he took another book out of the pile.

"This is your writing text, spelling, grammar, stuff like that."

"I like to write," Alpha said. Her voice had a relaxed, friendly, and interested tone to it for the first time.

"Ugh," Beta said.

"Ugh to you," Alpha said. "I don't like playing checkers all day either, but I play, don't I?"

"I don't play all day."

"Girls," Tania said softly. "You have to pay attention to Mr. Richards when he is here with you."

They both pulled back as though slapped.

"And of course, there's science," Neil said, indicating another book.

"I like stuff about animals," Beta said. "We've got lots of books about animals. Let's show him, Alpha. They're over in the bookcase back there," Beta said, turning slightly to look behind her. The movement caused Alpha discomfort and she poked her.

"He can see them later. He's showing us his books now," she said.

"Of course," Neil went on, "I have materials on history. Later on, we'll get a screen so I can show you things on a slide projector."

"A screen? What's that?" Beta asked.

"A screen? Well that's a piece of white material on which we can project pictures," he said.

"She knew what it was. She likes to ask dumb questions," Alpha said.

"I do not."

"When is all this going to begin?" Alpha asked, ignoring her.

"Well, right away. I'd like to start by giving you some tests," Neil said, taking a folder out of his briefcase.

"I knew it," Alpha said, folding her arms across her chest defiantly.

"Tests, ugh," Beta said. "That's all we ever get." She folded her arms the same way.

"This is just to see how much you already know so I can know where to start with you." He spoke softly, patiently. It was, after all, his patience that distinguished him from other teachers.

The twins stared at him for a moment, but Alpha didn't look placated. Suddenly she winced and Beta slapped the arm of the couch. For a moment Neil had the impression Beta was merely Alpha's arm.

"We thought this was supposed to be different," Beta said to Tania. "You said he was different."

"He is."

"Then why is he giving us tests?" She turned to Neil. "You're not really a teacher from a real school, are you? You're just another part of this place, right?" Beta demanded.

"No. I'm a teacher in Centerville," Neil said calmly.

"No, you're not. You're just another doctor disguised as a teacher," Beta said.

"He's not lying," Alpha said suddenly, her gaze fixed on Neil. Then she turned to Beta. They looked at each other intently and Neil looked at Tania. She smiled and nodded. He understood that something was happening between the twins. It took only moments.

Beta relaxed markedly. She unfolded her arms and leaned against the side of the couch. Alpha turned back to him.

"We want to know about your school," she said. "We want to know what it's like."

"Okay," Neil said. "What kinds of things do you want to know?"

"We want to know about the other children—what they're like and what they do."

"Now Alpha, you don't tell Mr. Richards what he should teach and show you," Tania said.

"He'll do it. Won't you?" She turned to him and smiled, and for a moment he could do nothing but look into her eyes. He felt her and Beta's need to know. It was communicated to him so vividly, it practically became his need to know.

"Sure," he said. "I'll bring in some things my other students did over the years and I'll bring in some pictures of the school and the students."

"When?" Alpha asked quickly.

"Tomorrow," he said. Beta clapped her hands together, but calmed down instantly when Alpha glared at her.

"All right," Neil said, "why don't we work out our

daily schedule—what subjects we'll study when, and then we can get started on everything, okay?"

"I'll leave you guys for now," Tania said. She nearly laughed at the expression of panic in Neil's face, but after he began, and got into the texts and workbooks, he found himself relaxing despite the situation. It was as if the work was truly magical and did shut out everything else.

Apparently, it was the same for the twins. It wasn't long before they were asking good questions and answering some of his. He got them to take the reading and math tests, promising he would hold off the other tests for another day. When they began, he stood back and watched them work.

Even though Beta had an easy opportunity to copy answers from Alpha, she did not. She was just as intent on her own work, but yet he didn't get the feeling they were each concerned with themselves. Rather, he got the feeling they were more like partners, each doing her share. When they finished, Alpha collected Beta's first and handed both papers to him as though she were handing him her own.

Just before the session came to an end, Alpha turned to him.

"Why are you working with us?" she inquired.

"Why?" He looked at Beta, but now her face was locked in a gaze so similar to Alpha's they were truly of one expression. "Because you should be learning all this. It's what girls your age with your abilities learn."

"But we're not going to go to your school," Alpha

said. She looked around the apartment as if to say, "We're not going to go out of this apartment, ever."

"Well . . . it's not for me to decide what you're going to do and what you're not."

"We know. The doctors decide that," Alpha said as though reciting some gospel.

Neil was eager to end this discussion, so he pointed out the time, gathered his materials together, told them what to do on their own, and left the apartment. The moment he walked out the door, he stopped and took a deep breath as if he had been holding his breath for hours. He went directly to Tania's office and found her dictating some notes into a tape recorder. She stopped as soon as he entered.

"You're initiated," she said. "How does it feel?"

"Weird." He went right to the desk she had set aside for him and put down his briefcase. "You should have been there at the end. Alpha is very perceptive, but in an eerie way. It's as though . . . as though she knows a lot more than we think."

"Uh huh. What happened at the end?"

"She asked a very good question: why are we doing all this? In other words, what's the point?" He couldn't help the irritation in his voice. The initial experience with the twins had left him a great deal more unnerved than he had anticipated. "I couldn't help thinking that's a good question."

Tania sat back and studied him a moment. She saw the tension in his face.

"I think I know what you're feeling," she said.

"Do you?" He regretted the aggression and shook his head. "I just—just don't want to see myself as part of any cruel experiment. This place . . . people like Dr. Endermo and Dr. Henderson, keeping them alive in that . . . fish bowl . . . for what? Why are we doing all this?"

"Are you sure you're not looking for some excuse to get out of this now, Neil?" She sat forward, her eyes small, her own temper riled. "You've discovered you might not have the stomach for walking in there and working with those kids, so you try to make the whole thing look bad. Isn't that it?"

"I don't think so," he replied softly. *Maybe she was right*, he thought. "I don't know," he added.

The flush that had come into her face made her even more attractive. He liked the way her eyes flashed.

"Well, I don't think of myself as part of some cruel experiment. I'm no mad scientist working with freaks."

"No, I didn't mean you," he said, trying to effect a retreat. "I meant . . . well, why is this all being done? I never really got Endermo to explain the purpose in great detail."

"Look," she said, sitting back calmly. "It's through mistakes, the unusual occurrences that take place that we learn about ourselves and our world. The abnormal have a lot to tell us about the so-called normal."

"What?" He smiled. "That sounds like scientific double talk."

"No, listen." She stood up and walked around her

desk, carrying a pencil in one hand which she used
to punctuate ideas like a college lecturer. "Did you
ever read Pike's work on crowding and the human
condition?"

"I've heard of it, but no, I haven't."

She went to her book shelf and took a book down.
She thrust it into his hands as she walked past him,
still talking like a college professor as she did so.

"Well, everyone knows what kind of population is
being predicted for the world in the twenty-first
century, the overcrowding, the great masses of
humanity that will be, that we already have in
certain parts of the world."

"And?"

"And how is all this going to change humanity?
What will it be like for people to live in housing
designed like beehives? What kind of psychological
and emotional problems will be created? How do
you feel when you're crowded in a subway or an
elevator, for example? Just imagine living in those
conditions for most of your day."

"You think the twins will give you answers to
those kinds of questions?"

"In a way, yes. Don't you see how that's possible?
No two people could live closer together," she
replied. He nodded.

"Yes, I see what you mean."

"So?" she asked, smiling. She held her hands out
as though the conclusion was always that obvious.

"But are they two people? I mean, I understood
what Dr. Henderson meant by their having two
brains and being somewhat independent, yet

doesn't their condition change all that in a way that is so freakish it can't have any significance for us?"

"There is definite scientific value to this project," she said with a determined look in her face. "Believe me, I wouldn't be in it otherwise. Nobody could care for those kids more than I do. I mean, where else would you have them? A circus?"

"Of course not."

"So? They're getting the best medical care possible and with the intent psychological counseling I'm providing, they're not being abused. They're being studied . . . under microscopes, as you say, but not abused. I wouldn't stand for them being abused. And now you're going to help educate them so they can understand more about the world they were born into and more about themselves. It's not so much unlike the purposes for educating anyone."

"Except what will they do with the education? That's what Alpha wanted to know."

"Frankly, I can't answer that right now. Let's go one step at a time. Obviously, there's good reason to move slowly. You'll admit to that, won't you?"

He nodded.

"Good." She squeezed his upper arm gently and smiled. "You can do this. I know you can."

"I wish I had your confidence. Anyway, I'm sorry I came at you so hard."

"It's okay." She smiled.

"No," he said, "I've got to make up for it." He looked at his watch. "I know . . . what do you say to my taking you out for a real lunch, cocktails and all. We've got to celebrate my initiation anyway," he added quickly.

"Very sneaky." She put her hands on her hips and nodded. "No wonder Dr. Endermo drafted you."

"Does that mean you'll go?"

"Purely to celebrate your initiation. We'll call it a working lunch."

"Great. I'll bring a notebook."

They both laughed, releasing the tension. To Neil it felt as though air had been drained from an overblown tire, one that had been about to explode, and as soon as they left the compound, he felt even more relief.

It was a particularly bright and warm early July day, yet it wasn't until he had driven down the long driveway that he noticed how vibrantly blue the sky was and how vividly white the soft, cotton candy clouds. He suddenly realized that this was something the twins had never seen and probably never would. Their entire world was that apartment, an apartment with no windows to the outside. *Perhaps they would be better off in a circus*, he thought.

Tania had suggested a place called Goody's off Route 52 just outside of Woodbourne. Goody's was a small place with a casual intimacy that he liked. Even though the tables were relatively close together, people were into their own conversations so firmly, they didn't intrude upon one another. He and Tania were seated practically in the middle of the room. Four waiters rushed about with amazing dexterity, threading themselves in and out of the

small aisles, bringing people the delicatessen sand-
wiches for which Tania said Goody's was famous.

"This is rather crowded and we don't have that
much space, yet I don't feel annoyed or put-upon.
Why is that, Doc?" he asked her after they were
seated and handed menus.

"Concentration. The ability to shut out sights and
sound—auditory and visual discrimination. People
develop it more in urban areas. Public works em-
ployees can be working with a jackhammer on a
sidewalk or road just outside people's apartments
and the people won't even notice. Really. Afterward, they can be asked about it and they won't be
able to tell you when the workers were there or
how long they were there. They shut it out," she
said, making the answer sound so obvious.

"And this is what the twins are doing to exist,
isn't it? Shutting out the oppressive closeness," he
said. Her smile faded.

"I used to think so, yes."

"And now?"

"And now I think they feed on the closeness. I
think they're merging."

"Merging? How do you mean?"

"I really would like to wait for your impressions.
Since you'll be the one other person working so
closely with them, I will value your opinions," she
said.

"Maybe it's better if I have something to look for.
I'm no psychologist, you know. I'm just a small
town school teacher who got tapped for an unusual
experience. I'm still unclear why me."

"You don't appreciate your talents, Neil. You're a specialist in your field, and that's what Dr. Endermo and the team were looking for. What is so hard to understand? An ordinary teacher or a teacher who deals only with normal children would be out of his or her league."

"Anyone would be, considering this," he said.

"Granted, but less so for you. Okay. Mystery ended," she said and studied her menu. "Roast beef is great here."

"I'll tell you what I think after only one visit," he said, refusing to leave the topic. She lowered her menu. "You asked me before if I thought they were really two people. I think they're like two parts of one personality . . . schizophrenic in a weird sense. All of us have Beta's childish innocence, but all of us also develop Alpha's skepticism. The differences were so sharp and yet they co-exist, just like two parts of one personality."

"That's very perceptive of you. It took me a few months to come to that conclusion. You see, you've already answered your own question—that's why you were logical for such a job." He nodded thoughtfully. "Now back to the roast beef." She lifted the menu again.

"What did Alpha mean by other kids like them? Why does she think that?"

"My guess is she is voicing a need to have others like herself so she doesn't feel as freakish. It's reassuring to find out that other people suffer from the same illnesses or problems, that there are other people who are too short or too tall or too thin or too fat," she said without lowering the menu.

"Did you or one of the other doctors ever go into what is exactly wrong with them and show them examples of others?"

"I haven't, no, and I don't believe anyone else has." She lowered the menu and smiled. "What are you going to order?"

"You know," he said, ignoring her question, "for a few moments in there, I felt intimidated by Alpha."

Tania stared at him, then leaned forward, her face so close to his, he could see the little veins just under her eyes.

"Do you mean you saw things from her point of view?"

He thought for a moment.

"Yes," he said. "I did. Identifying with the needs of your students isn't such a rare thing, but this was different, this was almost as if . . ."

"As if you heard her thoughts."

"Yes," he said excitedly.

Tania nodded and sat back.

"The roast beef is great," she repeated and that was what he ordered when the waiter came to their table. No matter how he tried to direct the conversation back to the twins and the weird feelings he had in their apartment, Tania sidestepped and talked about something else.

"I thought this was going to be a working lunch," he finally said. "Why are you avoiding some of my questions and comments?"

"Am I?"

"There's something else going on in there, something neither you nor Dr. Endermo have told me. Am I right?"

She stared at him without speaking. Then she nodded slowly.

"They haven't even told me," she said. "But I feel it, too. That's why I was so glad they finally brought in another outsider. I'm depending on you to hang in there, Neil."

"Well . . . what do you think it is?"

"I don't want to say anything yet. I want to wait until you've had more experiences with them, okay?"

"You sure this isn't a psychologist's gimmick to keep me on the job?"

"See," she said, half joking, "you're already a member of the research team. You won't believe anything unless it's validated. Welcome to Mandicott."

He laughed and their lunch conversation moved on to more ordinary things. They talked about films and books and places they had both been. Once they left the topic of the twins, they both seemed to relax. He enjoyed her company, and even though she maintained that element of aloofness, he continued to hope something more might develop between them.

As they drove back to the institute, they both grew quiet. It was as if the closer they came to the project, the more introspective they became. Clouds had slipped over the sun and cast a dark shadow over the road ahead of them. It looked like a potential thunderstorm by the time they passed through the front gate. The first drops sent them rushing toward the entrance.

After they entered the building, he returned to the twins' apartment for their afternoon session. They were seated on the same place on the couch as if they hadn't moved since he was gone. He pulled a chair up to the table in front of them. Then he sorted out his materials, trying to appear as businesslike as possible.

All the while he was aware of Alpha's hard gaze and Beta's constant smile. They were quiet and patient, like well-trained animals. It unnerved him. The kids in his class back at school were continuous personifications of unchecked energy—sliding chairs, talking quickly, touching and punching one another. He had learned quickly that good preparation and organization were the keys to success with them. They couldn't tolerate long delays.

"Now," he said, "I've been looking at these samples of your writing . . ."

"Why do you want to teach us, Mr. Richards? Why don't you want to teach your other students?" Alpha demanded. Indeed it was as if she had been sitting there on pause after that final question from the first session, and his reappearance had triggered her again.

"Aren't your other students going to be upset?" Beta added quickly. He looked from one to the other.

"Well, I'm on what's called a leave of absence. I'll be able to go back."

"When?" Alpha asked. There was such an authoritative tone to her voice that it was difficult for him to think of her as only twelve.

"When I'm finished," he said, forcing a smile.

"You mean when something happens to us?"

"No, I don't mean that."

"Then how can you be finished? Don't we have to keep learning things?" she insisted.

"Of course. It's just that . . . well, they'll bring in another teacher, I'm sure."

"Why not keep you?" Alpha asked and smiled as though she already knew the answer.

"Now look," he said, sitting back. "I don't know everything about this project. They hired me to help you and I'm here to do that now," he said, amazed at how quickly he had become defensive.

Alpha continued to scrutinize him for a moment, then looked down at the papers. He felt he had gotten past some obstacle and went back to the topic.

"Now then. You both seem to know what a sentence is, but many times you forget to punctuate when you stop. For example, here on Beta's paper . . ."

"Why my paper! Why not hers? She forgets, too."

"I know. I just wanted to show you what I meant," he said softly. Beta still looked wounded.

"Use mine," Alpha said quickly.

"All right. We'll use Alpha's. Here Alpha should have placed a period and capitalized this word," he said, pointing to her paper.

"Are there any more mistakes?" Beta asked happily.

"Well, there are spelling errors on both your papers. I'm going to prepare a spelling list for you, and when you have a chance, you can test one another."

"We don't have to test one another, Mr. Richards," Alpha said. "If I learn it, she'll learn it. That is," she added, turning to Beta and smirking, "if I want her to."

"Well, I hope you'll always want her to," Neil said. He noticed how intently Alpha was staring at him now. "Okay?"

"You like Miss Weber, don't you?" she asked him suddenly.

"Like her? Sure. Don't you?"

"You like her a lot . . . like a man is supposed to like a woman," Alpha said as if repeating something she had read in a textbook.

"Oh, well, we've just gotten to know each other."

"You wish she liked you more, don't you?" Alpha continued, talking like a gypsy fortune teller.

"Let's get back to our work here," Neil said.

Alpha turned away from him. She stared at herself in the wall mirror, then closed her eyes. Her forehead creased either from the intensity of her thoughts or a pain. It only took a moment, then she looked back, a wide smile on her face. Beta giggled and brought her hands to her mouth to subdue it. Then Alpha looked at her intently and she turned serious again.

"What's going on here?" Neil asked. "You two have something up your sleeves."

"Up our sleeves?"

"Planning something," Neil explained. He looked at Beta and saw the way she watched Alpha. She seemed to be waiting for some confirmation.

"I just wished for something. That's all," Alpha said.

"Alpha gets all her wishes," Beta said. "Tell him some of your wishes, Alpha."

"I'm tired," Alpha suddenly said. She closed her eyes and leaned back on the couch.

"Oh? I thought we would . . ."

Alpha opened her eyes, which did look tired.

"Need to sleep," she said.

"Okay. Maybe we've done enough for the first day," he said, impressed with how the look of fatigue traveled from Alpha's face to Beta's. *Perhaps they had been working all the time I was at lunch with Tania,* he thought, *and that, plus the morning session, had tired them.* Their demeanor was making him nervous. Perhaps they were a great deal more fragile than he had been told. He would feel terrible if he caused something to happen the very first day on the job.

He watched them rise from the couch and head toward the bedroom, their arms about one another. From the rear Alpha looked like a whole person being carried like a baby. He waited a moment, then looked in on them. They were already asleep in the bed, the blanket brought up to their necks, disguising their deformity and giving them the appearance of any two twins side by side. He stared at them a moment, then left the apartment, wondering if there was some other cause for their sudden fatigue, and if there was a reason, why Dr. Henderson hadn't warned him about it.

4

Neil hurried down the corridor to Tania's office to report what had happened. He opened and closed the door quickly, disappointed that she wasn't there. For a moment he wondered if he should phone Dr. Endermo. He decided it was a good precautionary move and went to Tania's desk to dial Endermo's extension. Endermo picked up immediately.

"Yes, this is Dr. Endermo," he said in a soft voice.

"Dr. Endermo, Neil Richards. I just came from my afternoon session with the twins and I had to end it abruptly because they suddenly became so tired, they couldn't go on."

"Uh huh," he said, his voice hanging, an indication he expected to hear something more significant.

"Well . . . the way the fatigue came over them . . . instantly . . . I thought . . ."

"Oh, I wouldn't concern myself with that, Neil. Didn't Dr. Henderson tell you that they could become tired quickly, from time to time? It has to do with their unique physiology."

"No, as a matter of fact, he made it sound as if they would be better students than my present class of handicapped children."

"Well, I know he was referring to their ability to learn. You'll find that extraordinary. Don't concern yourself with this. It was their first time with you. You'll arrive at a workable schedule with them soon, I'm sure. Was it interesting for you?"

"Oh sure. It's not that."

"That's good then," Endermo said quickly. "Tell you what I'll do, though. I'll have Dr. Henderson check on them now, and I'll let you know if there is anything wrong."

"Fine."

"Don't hesitate to call if there is anything else, no matter how insignificant it might seem, Neil."

"Thank you."

"Not at all. Thank you for being so concerned. 'Bye now."

Neil cradled the phone slowly and sat back in Tania's chair. He closed his eyes and pressed his thumb and forefinger on his temples. Tension made his head feel heavy. A moment later he heard the office door open and opened his heavy eyelids to see Tania step in. He was immediately taken by the way she smiled and gazed at him. There was a remarkable change in her entire demeanor. She looked softer, much more relaxed, even seductive. Her lips were wet, her face flushed. She wasn't wearing her suit jacket and her blouse was unbuttoned right down to the top of her cleavage.

"Hi," she said, her voice almost a whisper. She leaned back against the door, her hands behind her. He heard the door lock click shut.

"Hi." He smiled with confusion. "The twins got very tired," he began, but stopped as she started toward the desk. She had pulled her shoulders back so her bosom lifted against her cotton blouse and the unbuttoned shirt opened enough to reveal the tops of her breasts. Despite his effort at self-control, her movements and appearance sent a tingle down his spine that warmed his whole body and turned up the inside of his thighs. His erection began building even before she reached him; he pulled himself closer to the desk to hide it. She pushed some papers away and sat on the desk, just in front of him.

"I'm glad," she finally said.

"Huh?"

"Brought you here earlier," she whispered. "I've been hoping we would have some time together, to really be together."

"Is that so?" His smile widened. "What's going on?"

"Can't you tell?" she asked and reached out to run her hand over his head and down the left side of his face, taking time to trace the curve of his ear with the tips of her fingers that settled finally on his neck.

"Tania?" he said as if he had to be certain it was really her.

"Yes," she said, and pressed her fingers against his neck so he would lean forward as she brought her lips closer to him. Her unbuttoned blouse opened even more. First she kissed his forehead, then she pressed his face against her bosom. He inhaled the delicious scent of her cologne and felt the softness of her breasts. He heard her moan and when he tried to pull back, he was surprised at how firmly she held him to her.

Finally, he reached out, took her at the waist, and lifted her off the desk and away from him.

"What's going on?"

He liked her; he wanted her. He was quite aroused, but there was something so bizarre about the abruptness of her behavior that he couldn't accept it.

She simply smiled.

"Can't you tell?" she said, sounding more like a flirtatious teenager than the mature, intelligent woman he had begun to know.

"But why . . . all of sudden . . . and like this? I thought you wanted to keep our relationship professional for a while."

"It's professional," she said, moving back to him. She ran her fingers inside his shirt and started to unbutton it.

"Now wait a minute . . . this is your office. What if someone came by?"

"The door's locked. No one will come by."

"But . . ." He looked at the couch. He couldn't deny he wanted to make love to her, and she was as warm and as beautiful as he imagined she could be, but there was still something about her that not only made him hesitate; it actually frightened him.

He had known aggressive women. There was that physical education teacher last year, the one who didn't make it through the semester. He had taken her out and she had brought him right to her apartment and practically raped him. Afterward, he found out he was one of many, not only that month, but that week. The school board found out about her, too.

Right now, Tania reminded him of her, but he sensed this wasn't what she was really like. Why was she doing this?

She was pressing her tongue into his ear. Her left hand was on his thigh and moving quickly toward his now-firm erection. She passed over it and moaned again. Then she began fumbling with his belt buckle.

"Tania, wait . . ."

She didn't seem to hear him. Her eyes were closed and she was lifting her lips to his.

It took all the self-control he could muster. Later on, a part of him would chastise him for turning her away, but there was a better part of him that demanded it, that told him if he really cared about her, he would not take advantage. For that's what it had begun to feel like—like he was taking advantage. Why he should have these feelings, he did not know. She was a mature, intelligent woman. She wasn't drunk; she was simply driven to make love to him. Yet, it wasn't the way he wanted it.

"This isn't right," he said. "Something's not right."

He pushed her away and she grimaced with disappointment.

"Neil," she said. "I want to make love to you. I like you."

"I don't know what's going on," he said. He knew he looked ridiculously flustered as he moved away from her. He scooped up his files and rushed toward the door as though he were fleeing from a female vampire.

"Neil." She reached out toward him, holding her arms away from her body. Then she quickly went to her blouse and started to unbutton it further. "Come back."

"I'll talk to you later," he said. "When you're more yourself," he added and fumbled with the door lock. "'Bye," he added when he had it opened. He didn't look back, but he heard her cry out in disappointment.

He hurried down the corridor and out to the parking lot, actually moving like a man in flight. He didn't calm down until he drove out of the compound and headed for his apartment. As soon as he arrived, he poured himself a stiff drink and took a quick shower. Afterward, somewhat relaxed, he put on his robe and sat in the living room, sipping his drink and reviewing what had just happened.

He knew if he told any of his friends about it, they would think he was an idiot for the way he behaved and for rejecting her. Since he had first met her, he had fantasized that scene a number of times, but the difference was, he had romanticized her, won her over with his charm, his personality, his sincere affection for her. This was different; this would have been like making love to a woman sleepwalking through her own erotic dream.

That was it, he thought. She had a glazed look, the look of someone under a spell. That was what frightened him about her. What had happened to her? Maybe he shouldn't have run out on her; maybe he should have tried to help her. Now he felt guilty for leaving her. But if he would have remained in that office, something would have certainly occurred and afterward he would have felt guilty.

Maybe she had come to her senses after he left. *By now she was probably feeling foolish*, he thought. She was probably terribly embarrassed and was afraid of talking to him or seeing him again. It would make for some awkward first moments, that was for sure. They would have to talk it over if they were ever to work together again.

He was tempted to phone her. Separated by distance and the telephone line, maybe she would be more rational. But he decided it might be better to let more time pass. Instead, he made himself dinner and relaxed before the television set, watching the news. Just after seven, she called him.

"Hi," she said. Her voice had returned to that correct, almost formal tone. "How did it go today?"

"What?"

"The twins? Their afternoon session? I looked for

you afterward," she said, "but you weren't around
and one of the security guards told me you had
left."

"I don't get it. Are you pretending we didn't meet
in your office afterward?"

"Meet in my office? What are you talking about?"
she asked. She sounded so sincere.

"I was with you after I saw the twins this
afternoon, unless I'm going nuts."

"Neil, what are you talking about?"

"You're saying you didn't come back to your office
and find me there this afternoon?"

"Not unless there is a clone of me running
around."

He thought about the time, just when he had left
the twins, approximately how long he had spoken
with Dr. Endermo, and then her arrival. He estimated it no later than 2:10. He wasn't going to let
her pretend it didn't happen. She had to understand
he had feelings, too.

"Where were you exactly at two-ten this afternoon, then?" he asked as though they were in a
courtroom. She hesitated a moment.

"Two-ten? I had just gotten to the hospital library a few minutes before. I was reading an
extract I had ordered."

"Can you substantiate that?"

"Neil, what is this? You're beginning to frighten
and annoy me. Why am I on trial?"

"Can you substantiate that?" he repeated. He
could practically hear her fuming through the
phone.

"Of course. Mrs. Douglas retrieved the documents for me and was present while I was there. Should we call her to bear witness?"

He sat back in his chair. His forehead had broken out with beads of sweat. He didn't know how to begin. He found it increasingly embarrassing that she was pretending what had happened between them hadn't, but he knew he had to pursue it. How could he face her, work with her otherwise?

"Neil?"

"Could . . . could we meet for a short time? I think . . . I'm very confused about something."

"Of course," she said. "I'm still at the office. Do you want to come back here?"

"No," he responded quickly. "I don't want to meet at the institute."

"Why not?"

"I just feel different when I'm in there. I can't explain it over the phone."

"So then?"

"Could you come here? It's not really out of your way and . . ."

"Neil Richards," she said, her voice softening, "is this another clever way for you to get me alone?"

"After I talk to you, you'll see how funny that is," he said.

"Now you have stimulated my curiosity. I'm beginning to think I'm with a professional. You[r] dossier may not be as complete as Dr. End[er] thinks," she said. She waited for him to la[ugh]; he remained silent. "Okay. I won't [?] more. I'll be there within the half [?]

"Good. See you then."

He sat by the phone for a few moments. She could prove she was somewhere else at the time she was seducing him in her office? Was this simply a cover up on her part since he had turned her away? He felt positive she was embarrassed now and was simply trying to forget the whole episode.

He had seen her, touched her, inhaled her sweet scent, felt her lips on him and been aroused by her. How could that not have happened? He rose quickly from the chair and went to his bedroom to look at the clothes he had worn. Like a bloodhound, he brought his shirt to his nose and searched for her perfumed scent. On more than one occasion, when he had been with a woman, he had brought home her scent.

But he could smell nothing but his own cologne. What could he do to prove to her that this episode had indeed occurred and force her to face up to it? He reviewed every moment of the incident as he put on a shirt and a pair of jeans, but he could come up with nothing concrete to confirm what had happened.

When ⸺ buzzer sounded, his heart began ⸺ enly realized it would be he now ⸺ embarrassing position, forcing ⸺ ncident. How was he going to ⸺ ed the door slowly to confront ⸺ a slight smirk on her face. ⸺ here," she said. He stepped ⸺ nd she entered his apart- ⸺ entryway looking around for a few moments. "Traditional decor, just as I suspected." She walked farther into the living room. "And neat, again as I suspected."

"I'm predictable as hell, huh?" he said, an uncharacteristic tone of displeasure in his voice. He saw by the way she looked at him quickly that she picked up the note of tension, but instead of confronting it head on, she played her psychologist role. She acted very calm herself and sat back casually on the recliner.

"Comfortable," she said. "Can I have something to drink? A soft drink?"

"Sure." He went into the kitchen and got some cherry soda. When he returned, he found her completely reclined, her eyes closed. She had unbuttoned her suit jacket. For a moment he just stood there staring at her, appreciating the graceful turn in the lines of her neck, the way her nose turned up slightly and the emphatic structure of her high cheekbones. He longed to run his fingers over her face and gently trace each feature.

Suddenly he felt his hand begin to shake. The liquid swished in the glass. It was almost as if he were experiencing the aftershock of an earthquake, the earthquake being what had occurred this afternoon. For a moment he thought she had brought her fingers to her blouse and was quietly unbuttoning it as she kept her eyes closed, her head back.

Suddenly she opened her eyes.

"Neil?"

"Oh, sorry. You looked so relaxed there. I hated to disturb you."

"Just tired."

He handed her the soda.

"Thank you." She sat up. "Sit down. You look like a schoolboy about to confess he took all the cookies prepared for the party."

"Yeah. That's how I feel."

"I did see Dr. Endermo before I left to come here," she said. "He told me you called him and complained about the twins becoming abruptly tired. He told me to tell you Dr. Henderson checked them out and everything is okay."

"So I didn't imagine calling him from your office," he said. He looked at her as though that confirmed the rest, but she still sat with a confused expression on her face.

"Yes? Go on."

"This isn't going to be easy," he said, "simply because the conclusion will be that either you or I am going nuts. Maybe we both are," he added looking away. "In any case, you came into the office shortly after I spoke with Dr. Endermo."

"But Neil, I already told you . . ."

"Hear me out. You—you tried to seduce me."

"What?" The smile disappeared from her face and was replaced with a studied, clinical look. "Go on, describe it."

"Okay. You entered the office; you weren't wearing your suit jacket. Your blouse was unbuttoned and you came to the desk where I was sitting."

"How far did we go?"

"Not far. You embraced me, but I broke away and literally ran out."

"So much for my feminine wiles."

"No, I didn't leave because I wasn't attracted to you. The fact is it took everything I had to leave."

"I see." She sat back, her smile returning. "So you're still a decent man, is that it?"

"You're sure this person, the hospital librarian, can confirm you were in the library at that time?"

"For more than an hour-and-a-half. She even made me a cup of coffee, Neil."

He shook his head.

"I don't know what to say. One of us might be schizophrenic."

"Well, I guess I'm flattered. It's always flattering to hear you were the object of someone's fantasy, as long as that person isn't a psychotic."

"I can't believe it was just a fantasy, Tania."

"There's no other explanation, Neil. You must have fallen asleep for a few moments, had an intense dream, awakened, and left." She shrugged. "Hasn't it ever happened that you've had a dream and found yourself unsure whether or not it was a dream?"

"I might buy that as a credible possibility had I awakened in a chair and then left. But when I left the office, you were still there. I would have had to be sleepwalking my way out of that place. I'm sorry," he said, a little angry now, "but I'm going to have to talk with this Mrs. Douglas."

She stared at him a moment.

"Okay," she said. "Where's the phone?" He pointed it out and she went to it, first dialing information and getting the number and then calling Mrs. Douglas. He sat by watching and listening. He had to admire the way she controlled her temper and went about her business efficiently. "Mrs. Douglas, Tania. I have a favor to ask. It might sound silly to you, but please trust me. Yes. Thank you. I appreciate that. What I want you to do is remember this afternoon, the time I was at the library, how long I was there, and what I did. Yes. I'm putting someone on the phone. Please, tell him about that. And thank you. Just a moment."

She turned and held out the receiver. Neil rose from his chair and took it, slowly bringing it to his ear.

"Hello."

"Yes. Miss Weber was at the library precisely at 2:04," a very businesslike voice replied. "She had asked for an extract concerning sibling rivalry. She remained in the library until 3:35. At no time during that time did she leave."

Neil felt his throat tighten.

"Thank you," he said. It was like squeezing an unchewed piece of steak down his throat. He handed the receiver back to Tania. She took it quickly.

"Thank you, Clair. I'll speak to you tomorrow."

Neil returned to the couch and sat down dazed. Tania studied him for a moment, then returned to her seat.

"It wasn't a dream," he said. "It was different."

"A daytime fantasy."

"No."

"Neil, face it. What else could it have been?"

"I don't know," he said, his voice barely above a whisper. "But I'm confident it wasn't a dream."

She stared at him a moment. Then she leaned forward.

"Tell me about your afternoon session with the twins. Anything unusual happen between you and them?"

"I don't think so. I started working with them, but Alpha started asking questions about you . . . and me."

"Questions? What sort of questions?"

"Well, it's not unusual. Students often fantasize relationships between their teachers."

"She fantasized something between us?"

"Yes."

"I see. So the idea was planted in your mind then, and then you left their apartment shortly afterward, right?" She sat back as if that explained all.

"So? So what if the idea was mentioned in their apartment? How does that explain a detailed, vividly real scene?"

"Haven't you ever seen a mentalist at work? He or she places a thought in the subject's mind and the subject runs with it. On the surface it looks almost supernatural, but there is a good, psychological explanation for what happens. Same here," she concluded.

There was something in her face, something just beneath that psychologist's mask, something in her eyes that told him she wasn't just quoting textbook truths.

"Did such a thing ever happen to you?"

"Of course."

"In the institute?"

"And outside the institute, too. You're often unaware when it happens and when it doesn't."

"You make it sound like nothing," he said.

"Well, I'm not going to get all uptight about you now, if that's what you mean." She smiled and finished her soda. "I've got to be going," she said. She stood up. The images of her in her seductive pose returned, flashing before his eyes with such intensity, he had to close them and catch his breath. "Are you all right? Neil?"

"No," he said. She sat down again. He opened his eyes and confronted a concerned, clinical face, devoid of the sexual enticement he had just resurrected in his memory. "This is embarrassing," he said.

"You mean it's not stopping?" He shook his head. She leaned back. "Tell me about it. What just happened?"

He shook his head again and blew through his lips.

"Every once in a while now, I see you the way you were this afternoon, but it's not just a memory," he added emphatically. "You're standing here, in my apartment, but you're different." She didn't say anything. "Listen," he said, "something else, something strange happened to me at the institute. It happened the first day I was there."

"With me?"

"No. I was alone. I had just left Dr. Endermo's

office for the second time and I was on my way out of the institute when Alpha's face appeared before me, but so vividly it was as if someone had projected it on the air before me. She was calling me back."

"What happened?"

"I didn't snap out of it until I felt Dr. Endermo's hand on my shoulder. I was practically running back to the twins' apartment."

"Did you tell Endermo?"

"No, I just . . . I was embarrassed and confused and told him I forgot the way out. He seemed understanding and I left. I wanted to tell you about it, but we had just met and I thought you would think me nutty. Now, I don't know what I am."

"You're not nutty," she said. Something in her eyes told him that she knew a lot more than she was telling him. This realization made him feel like someone who had stepped into ice water. He sat back, nodding slowly to himself. She didn't move a muscle. She didn't even blink.

"It has to do with the twins, doesn't it? You know," he said when she didn't reply. "You knew all along." He looked at the telephone. "You just went through all this with Mrs. Douglas just so I wouldn't realize.

"But realize what?" he asked as if he had to discover the answer himself.

When he looked at her again, he knew she would tell him.

Tania decided she wanted some fresh coffee and

asked Neil to let her make it. He saw that she wanted to distract herself for a while, so he let the short intermission between them take place. He felt a strange mixture of relief and anxiety. He was glad that there was something more to the explanation of what had happened, glad that it wasn't some mental problem he was experiencing, and yet he understood that what he would hear was enough to disturb an experienced psychologist.

She set out two cups and saucers on the breakfast table just off the kitchen. He sat down and watched her pour the coffee.

"Cream and sugar?"

"Just cream," he said. She poured some cream into hers and stirred the cup slowly. He sipped his coffee but kept his gaze steadily on her.

"I didn't want to risk scaring you away so early on in your work with the twins," she began. She looked up, her eyes widening with her enthusiasm. "I was the one who pushed hard for them to have a tutor. When you asked me that first day why they had decided to do it, I was being truthful. I didn't know myself what had made them change their minds. One day, at a recent session, Dr. Endermo brought it up almost as though it was a brand new idea and everyone in the group quickly agreed.

"But I didn't care what their reasons were. My first concern was for the twins. It's always been for them. I know most of the others, maybe not Endermo as much, but most of the others, treat them like specimens, freak creatures under a microscope. But even in the short time I've been working with them, I've become fond of them, especially fond of Beta, as I know you will, too. You'll see."

"But what did you mean by not wanting to scare me away?" he asked, impatient.

"I was afraid that if I told you that the things that happened to you, happened to me, and were just as vivid and unexplainable, you might just hightail it out of there and leave me with . . ."

"With people you can't trust," Neil said, finishing her sentence. "That's it, isn't it? You haven't told anyone else these things. Why not? I would think it's all part of your work."

"Well, I did start to tell Dr. Endermo, but he made it seem so insignificant . . . he did what I just did to you, and then I thought if I insisted there was something more to it all, he might lose confidence in me and I would be dismissed. Believe it or not," she said, her eyes brightening with a determination that bordered on fury, "I don't want that to happen. I have my reasons. I really find the twins fascinating and the work I can do with them extraordinary. So I've kept a second file on them."

"I still don't understand why you didn't tell me any of this when I started."

"For one, as I said, I didn't want to scare you off, and two, I wanted a second opinion, an objective, second opinion." She drank from her cup.

"There's more, isn't there? There's got to be more. Something else than just you and I having vivid illusions while working with the twins. You might as well tell me all of it." She nodded.

"I didn't give you all of my predecessor's papers

and notes. What you read were her early conclusions. She began to suspect other things about Alpha. She realized there had been more than just a rare form of physical conjoining; there was a mental conjoining as well. Even as an infant Alpha was passing information between them telepathically."

"I sensed something like that, but I just thought it had to do with their physiology."

"In the beginning, her ability to do so was uneven," Tania went on, "but Jessup noted she was improving with age."

"What about Beta?"

"Neither Jessup nor I believe she has Alpha's power. Maybe it has something to do with Alpha's greater intelligence. There is so much to learn about them yet."

"Then all that stuff you were telling me about studying the effects of closeness on people . . . all that other stuff was hogwash?" Neil asked.

"Oh, no, Neil. That's part of it. Actually, that's my biggest concern and involvement in the project. Nothing I told you was untrue. I just didn't tell you it all outright because—because . . ."

"Because you didn't want to scare me away. I know. But I don't believe it. Why wouldn't you think this was just as fascinating for me?" He continued to study her. "There's something going on, something that frightens you, isn't there?"

She put her coffee cup down.

"You might as well know it all now," she said. "First, I found it odd in the beginning and still find it odd that no one else in the group has ever brought up Alpha's abilities. I've tried to get them to talk about it by making certain suggestions, but no one has picked up on them yet. Most of the time, they act as if they haven't heard what I said or read what I've written."

"Well, they might not put any stock in these ideas, scientists . . ."

"And second, Mary Jessup choked to death just after she started to come to these same conclusions about Alpha."

He held his coffee cup frozen in the air before him.

"What are you suggesting?"

"I inquired about the stove and Mrs. Gerhart's death. The maintenance man told me he couldn't find anything wrong with it, no reason for it to short out and electrocute her."

"You think Alpha . . ."

"I don't know what to think just yet, Neil. No one else seems concerned with these events."

He shook his head. Then something occurred to him.

"The first day Dr. Endermo took me to the observation room to observe them, he received a shock when he went to turn the door knob on the way out. I thought it was rather severe for a friction shock, but he didn't make anything of it."

"She didn't want you to leave so quickly," Tania said softly. "I think," she added.

"Then when I thought she was looking at me through that mirror, she was? She sensed me?"

"I think she can do that, yes."

"And affect the people around her, cause things to happen to them, cause them to do things?"

"That's my theory."

"If you're right, this is very dangerous. Why don't you just leave?"

"Because if there is something evil about her, I want to demonstrate it beyond a doubt."

"And then what?"

"I don't know, Neil." She sat back and closed her eyes, her face suddenly filling with fatigue. "Sometimes, when I think about them, I see a beautifully lit candle. I'm drawn to the flame, mesmerized, and I want to reach out, just like an innocent and unknowing child, and touch the light, unaware, unconcerned about how it will burn me."

"I appreciate that, but what's to stop her from doing to you what she might have done to Dr. Jessup and Mrs. Gerhart? If she indeed has these powers, she must know that you know."

"That's just it," she said, opening her eyes and sitting up quickly. "At first I thought that was confusing, and maybe she was just unpredictable, but now I'm beginning to think differently." She leaned farther forward and lowered her voice. "I think she's reaching out for help. I don't think she wants to be what she is, and I don't mean just conjoined."

"You're hoping, you mean."

"Maybe. Well," she said. "That's all of it. At least, all that I know. I suppose you'll resign now. I don't blame you." She got up to take the coffee cups and pot into the kitchen. He sat there watching her for a while. She no longer looked seductive in a cheap and obvious way, but she was still very attractive.

And he felt sorry for her. Despite her intelligence and competence, she was really alone at the institute. Suddenly there was nothing he wanted more than to be at her side, to be part of what she was doing; just as he had been filled with enthusiasm for the scientific and historic value of the project in the beginning, he was now filled with enthusiasm for working with her.

He joined her in the kitchen. She turned away from the sink and looked into his eyes.

"I guess I could run back to my safe classroom and put this all down as a bad dream, but I just can't walk out on you. Sounds corny, I know, but . . ."

The corners of her mouth softened into a smile. He loved the way her nose lifted just slightly as her lips parted. Her eyes softened and he felt the warmth radiate from her body to his. He kissed her in his mind before their lips met and the image joined with the reality in one long, ecstatic moment.

"I see you're not as predictable as you think you are," she said softly. "I like that. I like it very much. But you can understand now why I didn't want to have any romantic involvement, why it was so important for me to be focused."

"You don't have to worry about that anymore. I won't distract you at the wrong times. Promise."

She smiled and he kissed her again. Then, without speaking, they walked hand in hand to his bedroom.

"There's something that just occurred to me," he said after they were undressed and in bed. In the dim light coming through the partly opened door, she saw the smile on his face.

"What?"

"How do I know that this right now isn't just an illusion engendered by Alpha?"

"Oh, you'll know," she said. "I promise."

It was a promise she kept.

5

Neil hesitated at the door to the twins' apartment. He took a deep breath before reaching out to turn the doorknob. As he did so, he couldn't help recalling what had happened that first day Dr. Endermo took him to observe the twins. If Alpha indeed could send an electric current through that doorknob, she could do it now. According to Tania, there was a strong possibility Alpha caused the deaths of Mary Jessup and Mrs. Gerhart. Would she cause his because she sensed what he knew? Did she trust him and need his companionship as much as she apparently trusted Tania and needed her companionship?

Funny, he thought as his fingers hovered above the metal knob, I could end my life by touching this ordinarily benign object. Now that he was actually here and about to begin again with them, he couldn't understand his decision, regardless of how he felt about Tania. *How much of what he was doing was actually his own doing*, he wondered. He only hoped that if Alpha wanted him here and caused him to want to be here, she didn't do it to provide herself with another victim.

He turned the knob. Nothing happened except the door opened. He released the air he held in his chest and walked into the apartment. The twins were sitting on the couch waiting for him. They were dressed in a pair of jeans and plain, gray sweat shirts. They both had their hair brushed back and tied in ponytails. He closed the door behind him and smiled. Beta's warm and excited response was there, but Alpha simply stared at him with an intense expression of interest on her face.

"Hi," he said. "How are we doing today?"

"Hi," Beta said.

"Do you have the pictures you promised?" Alpha asked quickly. "Or did you forget them?"

"No, I have them," Neil said, and tapped a large, manila envelope he was carrying under his arm. "After our first lesson, we can look them over and I'll explain everything to you."

"We want to look at the pictures first," she countered.

"Well . . ." What he thought moved him was Beta's pleading eyes this time, instead of Alpha's threatening ones. "Okay, I guess if we get that over with, you'll concentrate better on what we have to do."

He pulled the chair closer to the table before them and put down his briefcase and the manila envelope. He had pictures he had taken with his previous classes, pictures taken for high school yearbooks and the school newspaper. In them his students were either sitting around a large, round table and staring with excitement at the camera, or sitting at individual desks and looking up, some smiling, some simply curious about the photography.

The twins visually devoured his photographs, hungry for anything that had to do with children their age. As soon as he handed them the pictures, they seized them eagerly and studied them with vivid intensity. Both scanned the pictures as if they were hoping to find someone they recognized. Beta touched one or two of the faces; Alpha's eyes narrowed. Quietly, without either asking the other, they exchanged the photographs.

"This was a class I had last year," Neil began to explain, "and that photograph is the same class a year earlier."

"Do they all do the same things at the same time?" Alpha inquired.

"Sometimes. Mostly, they each work at his or her own pace."

"The boys look funny," Beta said.

"No they don't," Alpha countered. "That's the way boys are supposed to look." She shot a glance at Neil quickly for confirmation. He nodded.

"Nothing really that different about them," he said. "Some have speech defects; there's a boy with dyslexia."

"What's that?" Beta asked quickly.

"He has difficulty reading. He doesn't see letters the same way a normal person does."

"Which one?" Alpha demanded. She pulled up the

corners of her mouth as if she were about to growl. Neil pointed to a blond boy seated at a front desk.

"Billy Davis," Neil said.

"He looks like all the others," Alpha commented.

"Oh, you couldn't tell about any of their problems by looking at them."

"Lucky them," Alpha quipped.

"Your room looks nice," Beta said. "What are all those pictures on the walls?"

"Posters. Some teach things; some are there just for decoration."

"I thought you were going to bring a picture of the school," Alpha said.

"Oh, sure. Here's one." He took out last year's yearbook and opened it to the first page. Then he set the book down on the table before them.

"What is this book?" Beta asked.

"It's called a yearbook. Every year the seniors are responsible for making it. It records all the school events, the classes, and tells about the seniors. It's something they'll have to remember their high school days. Every school does it."

"They took a lot of pictures of us," Beta said. "Maybe they'll put it in a book."

"Not like this," Alpha said. She turned to Neil and shook her head. Even though he wanted to, he resisted smiling, knowing it would hurt Beta's feelings. "She's such a dip."

"I am not. She's just saying that," Beta explained, "because we heard the word last night on television." She glared at Alpha angrily, but to

Alpha, Beta's anger was like flies on an elephant's back. She simply shut it out.

Alpha looked at the picture of the school, then at Neil, her eyes narrowing once again.

"What are these children doing outside the school?"

"Oh, that's a playground. The younger ones are taken out once a day for exercise. The picture was taken while a class was out there."

"There's no playground here," Beta said sadly. "They never take us out for exercise."

"They're out there every day?" Alpha asked.

"Every school day."

"We want to go see them," she said with determination.

"Yes," Beta added, clapping her hands. "We do."

"Oh, I don't know . . ."

"Pictures aren't good enough," Alpha said. She pulled her torso back against the couch and Beta did the same. They folded their arms across their chests and stared at him.

"Well, something like that . . . it's not my decision. You'd have to ask Dr. Endermo."

"You ask him for us," Alpha commanded. Then, after a short pause she added, "We can go and watch them without them seeing us and laughing at us."

Neil nodded.

"I'll ask him," he said with very little hope in his voice.

"You'll ask him and he'll let us go. You and Miss

Weber can take us," Alpha concluded as if it were a fait accompli.

"We'll see," Neil said. He closed the yearbook and put the pictures back in his case.

"Can't you leave those here a while?" Beta asked softly. Neil looked at her gentle, sad face.

"Sure," he said, putting the pictures into the yearbook. "You can have them for as long as you like."

"Thank you," Beta said, but Alpha continued to stare in silence. Neil felt the heat building around his collar again. He swallowed and took out his books.

"Okay," he said, "let's get to today's work."

He found them cooperative and interested, Beta perhaps a little more inquisitive than Alpha, who, from time to time, sat back and glared as though her mind was on other things. She was just as impatient as ever with some of Beta's questions and at one point during the tutoring, she turned on Beta and scowled with such vehemence, Beta's eyes filled with tears. After that, Beta was quieter and more subdued. At the end of the lesson, however, Neil found that she had absorbed everything as well as Alpha, or, as he surmised, as well as Alpha wanted her to absorb it.

"You told me yesterday that you could get Beta to learn how to spell a word if you wanted her to," Neil said, folding up the workbooks. It was his plan to learn about Alpha as subtly as he could. He and ̄nia had decided that they must not alert her to their private investigation. They had no idea how she would take to it.

"That's right," Alpha said with what he was beginning to see was her customary air of superiority.

"Could you show me how you do that?" he asked, smiling.

"Why?" Alpha asked. Skepticism and distrust seemed to come naturally to her.

"Maybe—maybe it's something I can do with other students someday."

"Why should we help other students? They'll never come here to help us."

"Oh, it's not that you're helping them so much as you're helping me," he said quickly.

"Show him," Beta said.

"I don't know," Alpha said.

"He brought us the pictures."

"I knew he would," Alpha said arrogantly. After a moment her face softened. "All right, we'll show you. Ask Beta to spell something hard. Make it hard," she repeated. She folded her arms across her chest again and pulled her torso into as erect a posture as she could.

"Hard, eh? Beta, how about spelling chrysanthemum?"

"Oh, that's far too hard. Even Alpha couldn't spell that." Neil looked at her.

"Can you, Alpha?"

"C r i s a n t h e m u m," she said.

"No, that's not right. I guess we'll need another word."

"Wait," Alpha said. "Write the word over here," she said, indicating an area to her left so Beta couldn't see. Neil leaned over and wrote the word, deliberately misspelling it to be sure they really didn't know the correct spelling and weren't conning him; he substituted an "i" for the "e." Alpha read the word, then crumpled the paper and gave it to him. She closed her eyes. He looked at Beta. For a moment her eyes became glazed, then she blinked rapidly. "Ask her," Alpha said.

"Beta?"

"C h r y s a n t h i m u m," she said. For a moment Neil said nothing. Viewing the mental telepathy chilled him. Alpha looked so satisfied with herself.

"Can you do that, tell her things like that, whenever you want?"

"Yes," Alpha said. "Can you?" she suddenly asked. He looked at her. Was it a serious question? Did she actually wonder if other people had this power? Perhaps she had been told so. "Can you do it with Miss Weber?"

"No," Neil said. "To tell you the truth, you're the first person I met who could do this sort of thing. It's a wonderful gift. You should always use it to try to help Beta. What about you, Beta? Can you send your thoughts to Alpha?"

"Of course she can't," Alpha replied quickly.

"I try, but Alpha won't let me," Beta said sadly.

"I don't want her thoughts. They're stupid."

"They are not."

"All of her thoughts can't be stupid," Neil said

softly. He smiled, sensitive to anything that might anger Alpha.

"It doesn't matter," Alpha said, quickly tiring of the argument. "She can't do it as good as me."

Neil nodded and continued to pack away his books and papers.

"But what you can do is wonderful," he said. "You can really help your sister a great deal. I wish some of my other students could do it."

She said nothing.

"Remember, we want to see your other students," Beta said, taking on Alpha's tone of voice and demeanor. When she spoke now, with Alpha sitting there so still, her gaze so fixed on him, he had the impression Beta was a puppet and Alpha was a ventriloquist.

Sure, he thought, a new possibility occurring to him. That's what Beta meant by "She wouldn't let me." Alpha had the capacity to override Beta's own consciousness whenever she wanted to and make her say and do things just the way a puppeteer could work a puppet. That's why Beta moved where Alpha wanted to move even though Beta was the one with the fully developed sciatic nerve. It was the most eerie and somehow disturbing thing he had felt about them. He suddenly realized that in a true sense of the word, Beta had been victimized since birth. Perhaps this was what Tania meant when she said he would feel sorry for her and like her more.

If he had learned all this in so short a time with them, Dr. Endermo and the rest of the team must know it, too, as well as more. *Why did they pretend to ignore it whenever Tania tried to bring it up?* he wondered. *Were they simply afraid people like me and Tania wouldn't want to work with the twins if they admitted to all this?*

"I know. I'll speak to Dr. Endermo about it," he said. "Okay. We had a good day." He looked at his watch. "Lunch time." He smiled at them. Neither returned it. Now they were both staring at him inscrutably. "I understand you have a new cook," he said. "Terrible what happened to Mrs. Gerhart, wasn't it?" he asked. For a moment he thought neither would reply. Then Alpha tilted her head slightly and smiled.

"Who's Mrs. Gerhart?" she asked.

"Mrs. Gerhart? I thought . . . wasn't that the name of your cook?"

"I don't remember her," Alpha said. She turned to Beta. "Do you, Beta?"

Beta shook her head, but he thought he detected a look of sorrow in her eyes.

"Oh. Okay. I'll see you later," he said, rising. Despite his desire to appear calm and unknowing, he felt he was fleeing from them.

"Don't forget about our trip to the school," Beta said as he started for the door. She was speaking in Alpha's voice again, behaving more like a duplicate than a twin with a separate consciousness.

"I won't," he replied, and from the smile on Alpha's face, he was positive he wouldn't.

Tania looked up expectantly and sat back the moment he entered the office. After he closed the door, he leaned against it and took a deep breath, then he wiped his forehead with his handkerchief. *Usually, I have to do at least an hour's worth of intense exercise to perspire this much,* he thought.

"You look a little white," she said.

"It's no good. I was terrified practically the whole time I was in there. I kept thinking that no matter how well I perform my act of innocence, pretending to simply be curious about this or that, she would read my mind and know the truth."

He plopped down in the soft, leather chair, dropping his briefcase beside him.

"I don't think she can do that so well yet, Neil. Her powers are still in a developmental stage. In fact, I've been thinking that maybe some of the things that have happened, things she caused, she didn't mean to cause. She didn't mean to go that far."

"I don't understand."

"She's like a young, but powerful ape. In its excitement it might grab something too hard and break it or kill it, but not mean to. Maybe she just wanted to stop Mary Jessup from asking the questions she was asking, and maybe she just wanted to punish Mrs. Gerhart for denying them something . . . a dessert, maybe. She doesn't handle frustration well. There's little compromise in her, but she might not know the extent of what she can and cannot do."

"Little consolation for Mary Jessup and Mrs. Gerhart," he said, but he had to agree, what Tania said made some sense. "One thing though . . . I

asked them about Mrs. Gerhart. I mean, I mentioned her death and said something like, wasn't
that terrible."

"And?"

"They acted as if they didn't know whom I was
talking about."

Tania nodded thoughtfully.

"Characteristic. Avoidance of guilt."

"I think Beta was forced to go along with Alpha's
act of ignorance. She looked more remorseful,
saddened."

"I'm sure. I told you Beta was more compassionate."

"One more thing. They want us to take them on a
field trip to my school to observe the children
during play time. They say the pictures I brought
them aren't good enough."

"Take them out of the institute?" He nodded. She
thought for a moment. "Do you know, this is the
first time they asked for that to be done?"

"You should have seen the way they went at
those pictures. Their curiosity about other children
is just natural, isn't it?"

"Yes," she said softly.

"So?"

"Of course, there's no way Dr. Endermo would
approve of such a thing."

"I know."

"Unless . . ."

They stared at one another.

"Unless she made him approve it," Neil said.
"She did seem confident about it." He shook his

head and sat up. "I don't think we have any choice. We had better go see the good doctor and tell him what we believe. Since we'll be going to him together and confirming what each other believes, it will carry more weight and you don't have to be concerned that he'll think you or I are imagining things. He won't think less of your capabilities because of what we tell him, Tania. Not now."

"I don't know. I wanted to have something more, some concrete piece of evidence. Especially before bringing anything more to the team. You don't know these people, how they analyze and nitpick. They can make you feel so stupid."

"Yes, but I just had her perform the mental telepathy with Beta. It was amazing," he said. She stared at him. "Surely they have done something similar by now . . . Dr. Henderson . . . some experiments. These guys are brilliant; they couldn't have missed this. They won't think we're off the wall. Frankly, I think it's getting to be too dangerous. It's too big a thing for you and I to handle alone. And there's no reason why we should."

"You're right, of course." She looked at her watch, then lifted the receiver and dialed Endermo's office. "Neil and I would like to see you," she told him after he answered. "It's rather urgent. Yes, thank you." She cradled the phone.

"He's going to stop in here. He was on his way down to see Henderson."

"Good." He thought for a moment. "I watched them closely while they looked at the pictures of my students and the school. There was such excitement in their faces. I felt so sorry for them. I know we're doing something valuable here with them, but I couldn't help thinking they were trapped, starving for sunlight, for the real sound of other children laughing. For a moment there, I imagined that the one-way mirror was like a microscope slide pressed over them, keeping them under glass."

"So you'd like to take them out, take them on a field trip of sorts?" she asked.

"Yes."

"Because you want to or because Alpha wants you to?"

"I don't know. Does it matter? It would be a nice thing to do."

Tania sat back, smiling.

"How you gonna keep them down on the farm once they've seen . . ."

"I know, I know. But that doesn't mean we shouldn't do it." He turned as Dr. Endermo came in and closed the door behind him. Although his pipe was unlit, he had it in his mouth. He wore his long white lab robe.

"Neil, Tania." He took the seat across from Neil, leaning back and crossing his long legs to get comfortable as he puffed on his pipe to get it lit. Tania waited until the small clouds of smoke began to rise.

"Thanks for coming right down," she said.

"No problem." He smiled and lowered his voice. "Anything to postpone going down to the dungeon. But don't tell Dr. Henderson I called it that. He's very proud of his facilities," he added. He turned to

Neil. "I've found that research scientists have little sense of humor about their work. Understandable, eh, Tania? Easy to psychoanalyze. Comes from their insecurity about their work, maintaining financing, the interest of bureaucrats . . . etc. So," he said, taking a long draw. "What seems to be on your mind?"

"I'm afraid we have something rather startling to tell you, Dr. Endermo," Tania began. "I've harbored these suspicions for some time now and I've mentioned or hinted at some of them at some of our sessions, but since no one else seemed to have these ideas and since no one has really picked up on them, I put them aside to wait for . . . wait for someone from the outside to come in and corroborate."

"I see," Dr. Endermo said. He smiled at Neil. "And that's what Mr. Richards has done?"

"Yes," Neil said. "Completely." Dr. Endermo raised his eyebrows and sat up.

"Go on," he said. "You've got my full attention."

"To begin with," Tania said. "I'm certain that Mary Jessup began to develop the same theories."

"What are these theories?"

"We believe Alpha has extrasensory powers. Not only can she transmit her thoughts telepathically to Beta, but she can do it to others as well. She's done it to us," Tania added quickly, "and I feel certain she's done it to other members of the team."

For a moment Dr. Endermo said nothing. He puffed on his pipe thoughtfully.

"Well, we've always thought there was something like that going on between the twins," he said, "but I must confess, this is the first time I am to understand that someone thinks she can do it with other people. I can tell you, she's never done it with me."

"How can you tell?" Neil asked.

"Pardon?"

"How do you know? She plants thoughts in your mind, thoughts you think are your own."

"Really, Neil, you think she can do that?" He looked to Tania and saw she wasn't smiling. "Well now, you'll have to tell me how you've come to make this conclusion."

Tania began by describing some of the paraphysical experiments she had run on Alpha: identifying objects and colors that were hidden from her view. She read him some of Mary Jessup's quotes concerning her conclusions about the telepathy between the twins.

"We've all known about that," Dr. Endermo said softly. "I've read your reports and Mary Jessup's, but the kind of extrasensory perception Alpha evinces in those studies is not really that unusual. I must say, I don't see . . ."

"We're sure she can do more," Neil said. "Affect people, change actions. Hurt people," he added.

Dr. Endermo didn't smile and didn't change expression.

"Why are you sure?"

"She's done it to us," Neil said. He looked to Tania.

"Before Neil arrived, it happened to me a few times. I was suddenly taken with images, thoughts, ideas that drove me to do things she wanted me to do."

"Like?"

Tania blushed, bit gently on her lower lip, then opened a notebook.

"I haven't even told Neil this yet," she said softly. "One day, while I was in there with the twins, Alpha became very curious about sex. She kept asking me about the differences between males and females. I tried to get her off the topic, but she was insistent. After I left, I didn't think much more of it. A young girl's natural curiosity . . . it was normal. But that very afternoon," she said, obviously having a little difficulty describing and confessing, "I went to the library and gathered some books on sex, deliberately searching for books with many illustrations. Afterward, I brought them in to the twins and gave them to Alpha."

"So?" Endermo said smiling now. "You said yourself, her curiosity was natural and . . ."

"But Dr. Endermo, I never remembered getting the books or bringing them in. The next morning, I found them there. I actually asked them where they had gotten them. I thought Dr. Henderson might have brought them the books. Beta said I brought them; Alpha stared at me with this self-satisfied smile on her face. I went so far as to ask Dr. Henderson about it. He acted as if I were crazy, so I didn't pursue it. Of course, I brought the books back to the library."

Dr. Endermo nodded. Then he turned to Neil.

"And what has brought you to these conclusions, Neil?"

Neil looked at Tania a moment. He couldn't prevent the blush from coming into his cheeks.

"Something happened between you two?" Dr. Endermo asked quickly.

"Yes," Neil said, and described the sex fantasy that took place in Tania's office, his belief it had actually happened, and Tania's subsequent proof that it hadn't. He told Dr. Endermo Alpha had been asking questions about himself and Tania in a very suggestive way during the session just prior to the fantasy.

"So you concluded she caused it?"

"That's right."

"I see," Dr. Endermo said. "Well, you might have something here, something for us to think about more seriously." He looked from Tania to Neil and from the expression on his face, Neil understood Dr. Endermo knew they were romantically involved. He had already discarded the sexual fantasy as just that. Tania looked at him and Neil saw she was making the same assumptions about Endermo's reaction.

"There's more to it," Tania said, unable to hide the frantic note in her voice. "We have come to the conclusion, not yet substantiated, that Alpha caused Mary Jessup's death and Mrs. Gerhart's death."

"Really?" Dr. Endermo's face turned grave.

"That day you first took me into the observation room," Neil said, "and you got that terrific shock when you touched the door knob . . . I think she caused it."

"You mean you not only believe she can transmit thoughts telepathically; you think she can will things to happen, generate electrical power?"

"Yes," Tania said. "The scary thing about it is it's like putting a loaded gun into the hands of a five-year-old. She doesn't realize her own capabilities yet, nor does she have a balanced sense of right and wrong. The way she is right now, she could kill someone and consider it as lightly as throwing a spit ball."

"Uh huh." Dr. Endermo remained skeptical looking.

"I wouldn't have told you these theories without more concrete evidence if it weren't for Neil," Tania said, "and his coming to the same conclusions."

"I see. There's no possibility of your having influenced him, is there, Tania? I want you to be objective about this," he said quickly.

"I don't believe so, Dr. Endermo."

"You haven't been able to explain Mrs. Gerhart's death, have you?" Neil asked. "There was nothing wrong with that stove, right?"

"Oh, there was. An intermittent thing, but nevertheless, a serious thing."

"But the maintenance man told me he couldn't find anything wrong with it," Tania asserted. "He said there was no reason for her to be electrocuted that way."

"What maintenance man?" Dr. Endermo asked.

"Sidney, the gray-haired man," Tania said.

"Oh. Sidney's a nice old fella, but he's really little more than a janitor here. I brought the head engineer over from the general hospital and he and his assistant traced the problem to some rather dangerously exposed wires. So much for building inspectors, eh? Apparently Mrs. Gerhart had dropped something behind the stove and when she reached in, her hands wet . . . well, it was a tragedy, but quite accidental."

"But Dr. Endermo," Tania began.

"No, hold on, Tania. I'm not saying I don't give your and Neil's ideas some credence. We're all scientists here and there's no reason not to make an investigation. Do you both feel endangered, is that it?"

"Well, we do and we don't," Tania said. "At this point it looks as though we have Alpha's confidence. I don't think she would hurt us."

"But on the other hand, Mary Jessup might have been thinking the same thing, is that it?" Dr. Endermo asked.

"Yes. Of course, we're being more careful with Alpha."

"Nevertheless, I don't like the idea of you and Neil being in any danger. Tell you what I'm going to do," he said. "I'm going to make this a priority. Discuss it with Dr. Henderson right now and get his opinion. If necessary, I'll have him run some tests. If there is any evidence that what you're saying might be true . . . well, we'll handle it from there."

"Dr. Henderson has never brought this up with you?" Neil asked.

"No, Neil. Not the idea of Alpha having the power to cause things to happen. We have discussed her mental telepathy with Beta and we have been running some experiments with her in that regard, but these other ideas . . . well, let me talk it over with Dr. Henderson. Rest assured, he won't reject anything outright. The man is the quintessential scientist."

Dr. Endermo stood up.

"Oh, there was something else," Neil said. "Of course, we'll wait until you make some decision about what we've told you, but the twins asked me to bring them pictures of my school and students, which I did."

"Fine."

"Now, however, they'd like to go on a field trip."

"Field trip?" Endermo looked at Tania as if he needed her to translate.

"Be taken out of the institute covertly and permitted to observe these children on the school playground," Tania said.

"You mean you gave this serious thought?" Dr. Endermo asked incredulously.

"I just felt so sorry for them," Neil said, "that I thought maybe you might find some way."

"Oh, out of the question, Neil. Really. The dangers to the project, to the twins themselves . . . they'll have to be content with what you can bring in."

Neil nodded.

"This was the first time they ever asked to be

taken out of the institute," Tania said. "Usually, in some way or another, Alpha always gets what she requests. I don't know how she will react to frustration on this scale," she warned.

"Now, Tania, let's not permit a preadolescent to blackmail us with her temperament. That's all she is, a preadolescent, despite her and Beta's unusual physiology. You've found that to be so even in your short time with them, haven't you, Neil?"

"Yes," he said. "They're both remarkably normal at times, but . . ."

"Then use the same psychology you use on your own students at school. I'm sure you'll be successful. But, don't do anything more with them until I talk to you after speaking with Dr. Henderson about all this." He opened the door, then turned around. "Hey," Dr. Endermo said, smiling. "Don't look so glum. It'll be all right, I'm sure. It's hard for me to believe that a scientist like Victor Henderson wouldn't have picked up on this quite a while back. I'm sure much of it can be attributed to coincidence and fertile imaginations.

"As far as what went on between you two . . . well, our special twins might be a lot more perceptive than we think, huh?" Dr. Endermo winked, then left.

"He didn't buy it," Neil said. "He as much as said he and Dr. Henderson wouldn't humor us, but that's what I felt he was doing. What about you?"

"I don't know. Maybe he's right. Maybe we *are* blowing this out of proportion. Mary Jessup could have simply choked by accident. Now they know what happened to Mrs. Gerhart . . ."

"But all that happened to us . . . the things you told him . . ."

"I'm not saying she can't plant images in our minds, but striking people with electricity, causing us to do things we don't want to do . . . I don't know. I feel a bit foolish right now and it's the one thing I didn't want to happen." She sat back and shook her head. "We should have waited. He's right. How could Henderson not know if Alpha can do anything like we think she can do?"

"Maybe Henderson does know but never told Endermo," Neil said. Tania looked up.

"What do you mean?"

"I told you my initial reaction to the man. I don't trust him. He's in his own world and I wouldn't doubt for a moment that he would even exclude his superiors."

"How are we going to determine that?" Tania asked. Neil thought a moment.

"If we have to, we'll find out ourselves."

"How?" she persisted.

"From Alpha," he said. "We'll win her total confidence and then we'll know it all."

6

Alpha and Beta stood by the door to the apartment and stared at the doorknob. They had done this once before, but had quickly retreated. Although Alpha wouldn't admit to it, she was just as frightened as Beta when it came to any attempt to leave their safe environment. What was really out there? What would happen to them?

But curiosity brought them back again and again. If their television set was indeed a window to the world, then there was so much for them to see and explore. The more they thought about it, the more they felt it was unfair of Dr. Henderson to keep them incarcerated.

Beta looked at her sister, then looked at the knob again.

"Go ahead, Alpha," she said. "Do it like you did the last time."

"What for?" Alpha said, pulling the right corner of her mouth in. "You'll just get frightened again."

"No, I won't."

"You will."

"You were frightened, too," Beta said. "Don't say

you weren't," she added quickly. Alpha shrugged. She looked at the one-way mirror, then back at the door.

"All right. I'll do it," she said. Beta took a deep breath and held it in anticipation. She watched Alpha narrow her eyes and concentrate on the doorknob. Nearly a minute passed and nothing happened. Then they heard the click, loud and clear. Beta clapped her hands with excitement and Alpha looked up with pride.

"I knew you could do it again. I knew it."

"Watch what else," Alpha said proudly. She looked at the knob again. Without their touching it, it began to turn. Beta's eyes widened as the door to their apartment swung open. "How's that?" Alpha said.

"Wonderful," Beta replied, her voice a whisper now. Her heart was beating madly. There was only one more door to go through and they would be out of their apartment, out of what Alpha now called their cage. "Are we going to go out?"

"Of course," Alpha said. "Why not?"

Beta nodded, her courage reinforced by Alpha's abilities, and started toward the outer door, but before they reached it, it opened and Dr. Henderson stood glaring at them. His teeth were clenched in anger, his eyes beady. He placed his hands on his hips.

"Get back," he commanded. "This very minute."

Beta retreated so quickly, Alpha bounced against her. Dr. Henderson closed the outer door and came through their apartment door, closing that behind him, too.

"Sit down," he ordered. When Beta didn't move, he raised his voice. *"Sit down!"*

They were on the couch in seconds, looking up at him. For both of them, Dr. Henderson had always been the equivalent of a parent. Since the day they were born, he was in charge of their lives. Alpha wanted to defy him, the same way a child might want to defy his or her father or mother, but she was afraid. She felt this way despite her vague realization that she could destroy him. It was the same as a lion and a lion tamer. There was no real question as to who would survive any struggle; she was just so used to his being in charge, something prevented her from going too far. He was the only real authority they knew. It was he who provided for them, who got them their clothing, their television set. Even Dr. Endermo seemed under his control.

"How dare you open that door? How dare you?" he said. "Didn't I tell you that was something you were never to do? Didn't I?"

Both girls looked down. Beta was the first to look up.

"We weren't going to go anywhere," she said.

"Don't lie, Beta," Alpha said. Beta was shocked by the betrayal, but it was something Alpha couldn't help doing. It was still important; it was always important to have the respect and admiration of Dr. Henderson, just as it was for a child to have the respect of his or her father.

"Well, we didn't go anywhere," Beta cried.

"Only because I arrived in time," Dr. Henderson said. He shook his head. "I told you what might happen if you disobeyed my orders, didn't I? What did I tell you?" he demanded. "Beta?"

"You said we would have to be separated."

"And what would that mean?" Dr. Henderson continued like some tutor encouraging his pupil to provide a complete answer.

"It would mean one or both of us would die."

"Alpha would die for sure," Dr. Henderson said. "It's questionable that you would survive. I told you," his voice dropping an octave and softening a bit in tone, "that there are people out there who would demand it, people with power. More power than Alpha," he added quickly to block that hope. "It would be out of my hands and you could never depend on someone like Dr. Endermo. You know that yourselves, right? Right?" he repeated.

"Yes," they said in unison.

"It's just lucky for you two that I came by. But I didn't come by accident," he said. His face reddened with anger again. Alpha knew what was coming even before it was said. She looked down. Beta remained attentive. "You've done something else, haven't you? Something you weren't supposed to do."

Henderson sat down and pressed the tips of his fingers together.

"When Dr. Jessup choked to death in here, I thought you might have had something to do with it, but I didn't pursue the matter. I waited. Then you went and killed your cook. And for what? For spite because I ordered her not to make you those rich pastries anymore. I covered up for you so that the others wouldn't demand an end to your existence, but you promised you would do nothing more to bring any suspicion to you, didn't you?"

"Yes," Beta said quickly. Alpha nodded.

"What did you do to the teacher? What?"

"It was Beta's idea," Alpha said quickly. "She thought it would be funny."

"It was not. She's lying."

"I don't care whose idea it was. It was another bad thing, another thing without my permission. I told you, nothing like that is to be done unless I tell you to do it. I don't want you getting into anyone else's mind unless I tell you to do so. Is that clear?"

"Yes," Alpha said. Beta nodded quickly.

Dr. Henderson leaned over and lifted Alpha's sweatshirt to expose the area where she was attached to Beta. He studied it a moment, then pressed his finger hard into her flesh and drew an imaginary incision down and across the bottom of her torso. She pulled back as if the tip of his finger was a flame.

"That's how it would be done," he said and sat back.

Both twins looked terrified. Henderson stood up and stared down at them a moment.

"It's time for a test," he said.

"Oh, do we have to? I'm tired," Alpha pleaded.

"It's time for a test. You wouldn't be tired if you

didn't play with that doorknob. Now go back into the bedroom and get ready. I'll return shortly."

He turned and left them.

"I don't want another test," Beta whined as soon as he was gone.

"Shut up," Alpha said. She glared hatefully at the doorway.

"But it hurts my head and it hurts yours, too. You said so, Alpha."

"We've got to do it," Alpha said, speaking through her teeth. She turned sharply, her eyes blazing with anger and frustration. Beta felt the heat and the terror. She started to whimper. "Be still," Alpha commanded. Beta nodded, drawing her sob back quickly. Then Beta brought them into a standing position at Alpha's command. She put her arm around Alpha and they started slowly toward the bedroom. They struggled to get their sweatshirts off, then lay down on the bed. They stared up at the ceiling, waiting.

"We're going to get out of here," Alpha whispered. "No matter what he says. We're going to get out of here. You'll see."

"I'm afraid, Alpha," Beta said, near tears. "I can't help it."

"Yes, you can. Just close your eyes. I'll fix it so you won't be afraid and I'll make you think only good thoughts, thoughts about the playground and the children and us going out there to watch, okay?"

Beta nodded and closed her eyes.

And just as Alpha predicted, visions of laughing children on swings and seesaws, monkey bars and sliding ponds came into her head. Her face broke out in a smile of contentment. And that was the way Dr. Henderson found them when he returned with his equipment.

The way Dr. Endermo was waiting for Neil and Tania in the hallway, Neil had the feeling someone had been watching them and informed him when they were leaving the cafeteria. He smiled and beckoned as they came up the stairway.

"I was just on my way to fetch you," Endermo said. "Dr. Henderson is waiting in my office. Have a good lunch?" he added in the same breath.

"I'm on my salad diet this week," Tania confessed.

"They don't do a bad job in that hospital cafeteria. How does it compare to the school cafeteria, Neil?" Dr. Endermo indicated they should walk on toward his office.

"Well, there's a lot more choice, of course." Neil didn't want to talk about cafeterias and food. He began to understand that Dr. Endermo had a technique of carrying a person into one digression after another, then bringing in the important points almost as an aside to catch one off guard. *Everyone's using psychology on everyone else around here*, Neil thought.

"Yes, I imagine there is. Well, here we are," Endermo said, opening his office door.

Dr. Henderson was seated in the left corner of the leather couch, as close to the arm as possible. It was as though he were trying to stay away from some invisible companion seated there with him. Here in Dr. Endermo's warmer and better-lit office, Dr. Henderson looked much smaller to Neil and far less intimidating. *There was something comical about him*, thought Neil.

Because of the thinness in his face and the sharpness of his nose and jaw, the man looked like a bird. His large, round glasses magnified his cold, analytical eyes. Now that he was seated, his large lab robe diminished him even more. It hung around him, draped over the couch, with his head protruding out of the aseptic white cotton material.

"Well, here they are, Dr. Henderson. Everyone be seated, please," Dr. Endermo said, and went to his own seat at his desk. "As you two know, right after I spoke with you, I went down to see Dr. Henderson and we discussed your theories and fears. He then proceeded to repeat some tests on the twins. I guess you had better explain that, Dr. Henderson."

"From the very first time we realized the twins had telepathic powers, we considered their ability to affect other people," Henderson began quickly. "For weeks at a time, I had Alpha and Beta hooked up to EEG machines and the like to measure their brain activity. When they were younger, I and my associates even encouraged them to attempt to do something akin to the things you feared they could do. They were unable to do so."

"Maybe they were afraid to show you they could," Neil said quickly.

"No, because they were too young to have those

fears and be that subtle. Also, they were eager to please us, just like infants eager to have the love of their mother. There was no deception and there was no extrasensory ability evident. Still, we monitored them and watched for any such development. As soon as Dr. Endermo told me about your fears and the reasons for them, I went in and ran some tests on their brain waves. There have been no changes.

"At this point I feel certain their ability to exchange thoughts is purely a result of their unique conjoining. No one else who has had contact with them has reported anything like the things you two have suspected."

"But Mary Jessup had these thoughts," Tania said. "I once brought her theory up at a meeting and you didn't even acknowledge the possibility, so I didn't pursue it."

"Mary Jessup and I spoke about it," Dr. Henderson said, smiling for the first time. "She even accompanied me during one of our tests of the twins' brain waves."

"I read nothing about that," Tania said. Henderson shrugged.

"By then she was probably satisfied that the idea was pure fantasy. To think they could make people do things . . . throw electricity through the air . . ." Henderson smiled even wider and shook his head. Tania blushed.

"But I know she did do things to me," Neil said. "She planted thoughts in my mind."

"Mr. Richards, you're a special education teacher

with excellent credentials and experience. I wouldn't venture into your classroom and try to evaluate your students. It's not my area of expertise."

"And I'm venturing into yours, is that it?"

"What Dr. Henderson means to say, Neil," Dr. Endermo began softly, speaking as if he were mediating between a problem child and his parent or teacher, "is he has the experience and the equipment to evaluate the twins when it comes to paraphysical powers, and just as you want him to have faith in your ability to teach special students, you should have faith in his ability to do what he does best."

"All right, how do you explain what happened to us, then?" Neil pursued.

"Neil," Tania said softly.

"No, I'd like to hear it from the expert."

"I don't profess to be an expert in psychology, Mr. Richards, but I think what happened is explainable," Henderson began, speaking through a smile. "Perhaps you were thrust into this situation too quickly. Maybe there should have been a longer period of orientation. The twins are fantastic; it is a world that seems a step beyond reality," Dr. Henderson said, his voice suddenly soft and reasonable. He looked at Dr. Endermo and Endermo nodded. "The mind plays tricks on itself," Henderson continued. "Here you were confronting these extraordinary twins who can send their thoughts back and forth to one another telepathically and an idea was planted in your mind . . . mostly by yourself," Henderson added, smiling. "Illusion gets confused with reality. It's a commonplace thing."

"I just can't believe that."

"I can show you all our test results, explain all the data, even bring you in with me the next time I measure brain waves," Henderson said.

It was on the tip of Neil's tongue to say he wouldn't know whether Henderson was telling him the truth or not, but he said nothing.

"In short," Dr. Endermo said, smiling, "we have concluded there is no danger for either of you to continue. Assuming that you want to continue," he added.

"Of course I want to continue," Tania said quickly. For a moment Neil felt betrayed. Tania wasn't challenging anything Henderson had to say. She didn't talk about her own extrasensory experience with the twins.

"If I might offer a bit of advice," Henderson said, looking directly at Neil, "it would be best for you to concentrate solely on what you're here to do. Educate them the best you can in the rudiments and fundamentals."

"But what for? What are they going to do with it? You won't let them step foot out of that . . ."—the word "cage" came quickly into his mind—". . . cage."

Dr. Henderson looked at Endermo.

"Neil, you remember when you and I first spoke, I pointed out the danger for the twins that would be inherent in their exposure. It's mostly for their own good that we keep them contained. But their health remains remarkably good and their existence continues. We're not pure, unsympathetic scientists here. For humanistic reasons, we thought they should benefit from some real education. Are you now saying you can't do this? Because if you feel that way, we'll make other arrangements."

Neil look at Tania. She appeared anxious, afraid he would end it all right then and there.

"No, of course I can continue," he said.

"Then do, but do it as Dr. Henderson has suggested. Keep a tight rein on your imagination and you'll enjoy the experience.

"So, I'm glad we had this discussion and everyone has been reassured that our twins are wonderful, but not supernatural," Dr. Endermo concluded. He stood up to indicate the session had ended. Tania stood up next, but Neil hesitated. He wanted to say more, to do something that would not end the discussion, but he couldn't think of anything. Henderson was staring at him, all warmth gone from his face again. Neil stood up.

"Okay," he said. "We'll stick to our own areas of expertise," he added, immediately regretting the spoiled-sport sound to his words. Dr. Endermo and Dr. Henderson exchanged a quick glance. Neil looked to Tania, but she looked away, obviously anxious to leave.

"Please don't misunderstand anything we've said here, Neil," Dr. Endermo said. "We appreciate your immediate involvement and concern with and about our special twins." He smiled. "This dedication you have to the job is precisely why Dr.

Forster recommended you and why we wanted you."

Neil nodded.

"Thank you. I appreciate that."

"And the twins are obviously comfortable with you."

Neil looked up sharply. *How did Dr. Endermo know that for certain?* he wondered. Was he observing him when he was with the twins?

"So don't hesitate to come to me with anything, even if you want to talk more about this."

Neil looked at Henderson and saw his dissatisfaction with Endermo's invitation.

"Fine," Neil said, tired of the discussion himself. "I better get back to the job."

"Talk to you later, then. And thank you, Tania," Endermo said, nodding as Neil and Tania walked out.

Even before Neil closed the door behind him, Tania was rushing away. Her footsteps hammered a hollow echo down the long corridor. Neil hurried to catch up with her.

"Why were you so tame in there?" Neil demanded. He pulled Tania to a halt in the corridor by taking hold of her right elbow and turning her around. "I began to feel foolish continuing the discussion."

"Because that's how I did feel, Neil . . . foolish. I mean, what were we offering up as evidence, when you think about it? Your sexual fantasy involving me. It's embarrassing."

"But what about that story you told Endermo, the one with the books on sex?"

"I don't know." She shook her head. "Maybe I did bring them the books and forgot."

"Huh?"

"I signed them out."

"Come on, Tania."

"He was about to end our involvement," she said. "Didn't you see that? The more we would have challenged and protested, the more he would have been driven to letting us go. He as much as threatened it. If we can't stick to our own areas when dealing with the twins, they'll get people who can. What would we have accomplished by losing our positions here? We certainly wouldn't have been able to do anything for the twins." She shook her head. "What can you say anyway when Henderson tells you the results of his scientific analysis?"

"He's lying. The man's not telling the truth."

"But why, Neil?"

"I don't know, but I'm going to find out. I thought that was what you wanted. I thought it was a prime reason for your wanting me to continue."

"It is. It's just that . . . I don't know, I'm so confused. I've got to sit down and think this whole thing out."

"I told you. There is only one way to get at the truth and that's through Alpha." He looked toward the twins' apartment. "We've got to keep working at gaining her trust. She's not going to like it when I tell her we can't take her and Beta on the field trip, but I'm going to tell her the truth . . . Dr.

Endermo said no. I was willing, but Endermo said no."

"He's probably right about it, Neil."

"You must not let them know you think that," he said quickly.

"If she has the kind of power we thought she had, why can't she simply make Endermo and Henderson approve the trip?"

"I don't know. Somehow they're immune to her, I guess." Tania smirked. "I don't know all the answers, yet," he said. He looked at his watch. "It's just about time for my afternoon session with them. What else should I do?"

"Let's think this out," she said. "Before we do or say anything more to anyone, even the twins. I have to catch up on some paperwork. I'll talk to you later, okay?" She started away.

He watched her go, then headed for the twins' apartment. He found them seated on the couch waiting. They looked groggy, their eyes glazed.

"So," he said, somewhat unnerved by the dazed expressions on their faces. "Did you work on the material we went over this morning?"

It took a moment for them to reply, almost as though it took that long for the words to register in their brains.

"No," Alpha said, speaking like someone who was under hypnosis. "We had to have tests and we didn't have time."

"Oh. You guys look tired."

"We are."

"Maybe we should skip this afternoon, then, and

let you rest. If you feel up to it later, work on the exercises from the morning, okay?"

"Okay," Alpha said. She looked at Beta and Beta brought them to their feet. He watched as they started for the bedroom.

It's as if they had undergone electric shock treatment, he thought. Maybe they had. Who knew what kind of procedures Henderson performed on them? He started to leave when Alpha called for him.

"Yes?" he said, coming to their bedroom doorway. They sat on the bed. Beta was looking down, but Alpha turned his way.

"What about our trip to the school grounds?" she asked.

"I'm afraid Dr. Endermo is against it," Neil said. "For now," he added.

"We'll go anyway," she said, then the two of them lay back against their pillows. In moments they were asleep. Neil remained there staring in at them. Then he walked to the bed softly and pulled their blanket up over them. He looked down at them for a moment. Suddenly Alpha's eyes opened and their gazes locked.

Almost immediately, he saw them seated in the back of his car, a blanket wrapped around them so no one could see what they were. They were looking out of the windows eagerly as he drove on toward the school grounds.

The vision passed quickly and once again he was looking down at Alpha. She smiled and closed her eyes.

Henderson is definitely lying, he thought and started out. A plan for smuggling the twins out and on a field trip began taking form, even before he was out of the apartment.

He found Tania in her office, not catching up on paperwork as she had said, but rereading Mary Jessup's papers. She looked up guiltily.

"Why are you back so soon?"

"They're exhausted. From Henderson's tests," he added, smirking. He stared at the extracts before her.

"All right," she said in a confessional tone. "I wanted to check something. I wanted to see if he was right about Mary Jessup deserting her theories after speaking to him."

"And?"

"As far as I can see, she never let go of the ideas. But why would they lie about all this? What's the point in not letting us know what the twins can really do?" she asked before he could say anything.

"Maybe they're afraid we'll leave the project."

"Can't buy that," she said, closing the extract and sitting back. "Endermo was about to cut us away in there."

"Then we go back to my original theory: Henderson isn't even telling Dr. Endermo what's really going on."

"But what *is* really going on?" She shook her head and stood up to walk to the window overlooking the parking lot. He came up beside her. "Did the twins cause the deaths of Mary Jessup and Mrs. Gerhart or didn't they? Can they manipulate people who come into contact with them or can't they? Why are they being kept alive and under study?"

Neil took her hand into his and she turned to him.

"I want those answers just as much as you do," he said. "Something has happened to me since I began with them. I feel drawn to them, even though I'm often afraid. It's as if . . . as if . . ."

"What?" Her eyes widened.

"As if they had a way of attaching us all to them. Understand?"

"Yes," she said, barely above a whisper.

"We've got to win their complete trust," he said with more animation. "You've got to help me do something."

"What?"

"We're taking them on that field trip."

"Oh, Neil, are you mad?"

"No. Tania, I don't care what Dr. Endermo says. Keeping them locked up in that cage all these years so they could be observed and tested is cruel. Yes, they have freakish bodies, but they don't have freakish minds and feelings. A part of them is very normal and demands some human contact. They need to see the sun, see trees, grass, and yes, see other children at play. We must do this," he said with a vehemence that brought a redness to his cheeks. "We must."

"I don't see how we can do it, Neil, and we might just destroy everything good we've been able to do with them if Endermo or Henderson finds out."

She went back to her desk. He watched her for a few moments and smiled to himself.

"I'm taking off," he said. "I need some fresh air and there's nothing more I can do here today."

"I'll call you later," she said. "I'll look in on the twins and see if they're able to do anything with me later. If I get out of here early enough, I'll make you dinner. How's that?"

"Sounds great." He leaned over and kissed her.

"You have such a strange smile on your face," she said.

"Do I?" He caught his reflection in a glass frame and had to admit he did. He shrugged.

"Neil, don't you do anything rash, okay?"

"Of course I won't. Talk to you later," he said, but after he left the office, he didn't head out to the parking lot and his car. Instead, he turned left and went past the entrance to the twins' apartment until he came to a doorway that led down to the basement. He moved quickly, with what looked to be an instinctive knowledge of direction. He had never taken this stairway nor entered this section of the basement before, so he didn't know why he should make one turn, then another with such assurance, but he did so.

Very quickly, he came to a double doorway that opened onto a back section of the parking lot.

Perfect, he thought and hurried on to his car.

Late that afternoon Tania called. Not only was he expecting it, but he was expecting what she would say.

"I stopped in to see the twins. They were tired, but we talked a little."

"I see. And?"

"You're right," she said, her voice suddenly very breathy. "We must take them on that field trip."

"I know. I have it all planned out."

"We'll talk about it at dinner at my place," she said.

"Great."

"About seven."

"I'll be there."

About 6:15, he got up abruptly from his chair because he vaguely remembered Tania had asked him to dinner at seven.

And there was something we were going to talk about, he thought, but try as hard as he could, at this moment, he couldn't remember what. He puzzled over it only for a moment, then hurried along to prepare himself for a nice evening with a woman he was growing more and more attached to, for more reasons than he could imagine.

7

Alpha and Beta looked up expectantly when Neil entered their apartment. He could see from the extra preparations they had taken with their hair and clothing that they anticipated a very special day. They had both brushed back their hair and pinned it with pretty, pink combs. Not a strand was loose and they wore their nicest pink blouses and a jeans skirt. Beta wore a pair of eggshell-color sneakers and white tube socks with a pink rim around the tops.

Neil stopped to consider them. It really hadn't struck him until this moment what it was he and Tania were attempting to do. From the second he had awakened, he was absorbed with the event. He reviewed their plan continuously while he ate breakfast, and again on his way to the institute. It was all to take place during his usual early session with the twins. That way there would be the least chance of anyone noticing their absence from the compound. No one bothered him during his sessions; no one interrupted.

When he drove in this morning, he went around

the building to that part of the parking lot closest to the basement door he had discovered. He backed up as near to it as he could without bringing any attention to his vehicle. The night before, he and Tania had discussed the route they would take, how long they would remain at the school grounds, and how they would return the twins. As soon as he met her this morning, he saw she was just as absorbed and intense as he was. They barely spoke about anything else. After a few moments, she entered the apartment, and she, too, was impressed with the excitement in the twins' faces.

"I'll get the blanket," she said without even addressing them. Alpha smiled slightly and turned to Neil. He could see she was intolerant of the slightest hesitation.

"You realize, of course, that what you will see are children who attend a summer session. It's really more of a recreational program than actual school," he continued. "Most of them will be younger than you."

"That doesn't matter," Alpha said curtly.

"I can't wait," Beta said. She clapped her hands. Alpha glared at her and her smile quickly evaporated.

"You've got to be very, very quiet," Alpha said. "I told you."

"I will," she said, pressing her lips together to contain her excitement.

"It's a beautiful day," Tania said, reappearing with their blanket. "Hardly a cloud in the sky."

"We wouldn't know the difference," Alpha said.

There was an adultlike bitterness in her face. In fact, both Neil and Tania thought she looked older, as if the anticipation the night before had aged her. To the contrary though, Beta looked younger, much more childlike.

"I know," Tania said sadly.

"Let's get moving. We're already ten minutes into my session," Neil said.

Tania nodded and took Beta's hand. Neil went out first and checked the corridors. They were as empty and quiet as ever, even more so because of the early hour. He knocked gently on the door behind him and Tania opened it. The twins came up beside her, both of them now wide-eyed. It was the first time they had looked out of their apartment. Whenever they had been taken to and from it before, they were unconscious. However, whatever Alpha now saw seemed to confirm what she already knew. She nodded to herself.

Neil moved quickly to the basement door and opened it. He looked up and down the corridor again, then signaled. Tania tugged Beta's hand and they began their short journey down the hallway. Beta held her breath. Alpha pulled her spine as erect as she could and looked ahead, her eyes small with determination. As soon as they stepped through the door and onto the landing, Neil closed the door and started to lead them down the short stairway to the basement corridor.

But Beta had trouble navigating steps. This was the first time she had ever confronted a stairway. Her timidity caused Alpha to wobble and for a moment it looked as though they would topple over in her direction and fall down the steps. Tania embraced Beta quickly to steady her. Alpha had to seize the banister.

"Easy."

"Oh, this is hard. I'm afraid," Beta said.

"Shut up," Alpha commanded. "Go."

Beta began again, moving down the steps like a woman of eighty, terrified she might fall and break a hip bone. Neil reached up to take her hand and guide her. Finally, all of them were standing on the basement floor. Neil started ahead immediately.

It was darker and cooler here. When he turned back, he saw how the shadows cloaked the twins, making their faces indistinct. They moved slowly, Beta not as sure of herself walking on floors outside of her apartment. She barely lifted her feet, shuffling along.

They heard a door slam to the right of them and Neil held up his hand to indicate they should wait and listen. Apparently, whoever it was had gone into a room. There was no sign or sound of anyone approaching. Neil moved as quickly as he could to the doorway that opened to the parking lot. When he reached it, he held up his hand, indicated complete silence, then opened it very slowly.

The twins followed the line of sunlight that sliced instantly through the basement corridor, fascinated by the sight of it. They both stared eagerly at the partially opened doorway, where a piece of blue sky was just visible at the very top. Neil peered out, looking from one side to another. Satisfied, he turned back.

"I'm going to get into the car and back it right up to the door. Just wait," he said.

"Hurry," Tania said. The realization of where they were and what they were doing was beginning to dawn on her. She was like a somnambulist beginning to approach consciousness. Alpha sensed it. She turned around sharply and gazed into her eyes, pushing her back to that half-conscious state she had been in all morning.

Neil hurried across the parking lot to his car. After he got in and started the engine, he looked to his right and saw whom he thought to be Dr. Endermo get into a limousine and be driven off. He waited until the vehicle was gone, then he backed up to the basement door. He got out and opened it, beckoning them outside.

When the twins confronted full sunlight, they stopped and brought their hands up to shade their eyes. They were like trapped coal miners who had just been liberated. The rush of fresh air, filled with the scents of grass and tree leaves, flowers and blossoms, was almost overwhelming. They both inhaled, then sniffed about like rabbits, turning their heads this way and that to catch scents that were really indistinguishable to Neil and Tania. Because they took them for granted and were so used to them, they were oblivious to them.

"Oh my," Beta said, looking up at the sky. "How wonderful. The clouds look so high."

Neil smiled at Tania.

"We've got to move along before someone spots us," he said. "And we don't have all that much time to spend."

"Hurry, stupid," Alpha commanded.

Beta, embarrassed by both her exuberant reaction and Alpha's disdainful manner of speaking to her, lowered her head and went forward, carrying them to the right rear door of the automobile. Getting them into it proved a little more complicated than Neil had anticipated. Alpha leaned over, making it awkward for Beta to navigate the opening. Tania and Neil guided them until the conjoined twins slipped through the door and were seated. Quickly, Tania threw the blanket over them, bringing it high enough to hide their conjoining. She got in beside them and tucked the blanket in behind their bodies.

"Looks good," Neil said.

"I'll ride back here," Tania said. He nodded and got in behind the wheel. In moments they were on their way out of the parking lot and the compound. Beta oohed and aahed at everything she saw, but Alpha remained quietly mesmerized by the world without.

"We're on our way," Neil said. When he looked up into the rearview mirror, the blanketed twins looked indistinguishable from any pair of twins riding in the back of a car. Confident they were going to get away with this and do a wonderful thing, he drove on. As the compound became smaller and smaller behind him, he relaxed, but it wasn't until it completely disappeared from view that Tania let out the breath she had been holding.

"We did it!" she exclaimed, and turned to Alpha, whose eyes were now bright and glazed, almost as if there was some sort of illumination turned on behind them. Even her skin looked different. It looked more metallic, although her cheeks were crimson from the rush of blood brought on by her own excitement.

Tania looked at Beta. To the contrary, Beta looked peaked, pale, her lips a little blue. The light in her eyes was diminished, dim. To Tania it looked definitely like Alpha was drawing so much energy into herself that she was draining her sister.

"Beta, are you all right?" she asked quickly.

"Yes," Beta said, but she took a long, deep breath.

"Alpha, is Beta all right?"

"What's wrong?" Neil asked, starting to slow down.

"Nothing," Alpha said quickly. She looked at Beta. "It's all right," she said, and pulled herself back into a calmer demeanor. Almost immediately, Beta's color began to return and her eyes got brighter. "She's just a little too excited, but she'll calm down. Won't you, Beta?"

"Yes," Beta said in a small voice. "I'm all right."

"It's okay," Tania said. "I think."

"Yes," Alpha said. "It's okay."

"All right," Neil replied, "then we go on."

This secondary highway into Centerville was sparsely traveled, but it was a relatively new macadam road. A county road crew was clearing the sides of brush. To the right and left was mostly undeveloped woods and flat land with an occasional house or two. After a few miles, they reached the outskirts of the village and more houses began appearing—modest ranch style and two story homes in developments.

The twins gaped at everything. Occasionally Neil looked into his mirror to catch the expression on their faces. Both looked fascinated, intrigued. Whenever a child or a teenager appeared riding his bike or near his home, they swung their heads around and stared intently.

"Coming into the village of Centerville," Neil announced. Tania smiled at the twins, who looked both terrified and excited now.

When they stopped at a traffic light, they all became a little tense. Drivers and passengers in other vehicles looked in at them. The twins faced forward, afraid now to look back at anyone or anything. The red light seemed interminable. Finally, it turned green and Neil shot ahead, made a turn, and took them down the side street that ran along the front of the school.

"This is it," he said.

"It looks like the picture, doesn't it, Alpha?" Beta asked. Alpha didn't reply. She gazed intently at the structure. Neil made a left and swung around to the side of the complex, bringing the car to a halt near a high chain link fence. Just on the other side of it was the playground. Right now, there was no one there.

"Where are the children?" Alpha demanded.

Neil looked at his watch.

"Should be coming out any minute."

As if on cue the side door of the school opened and the shouts of elementary school-age children spilled out to announce their impending arrival. Alpha and Beta leaned over to get the best view possible from their side window. Suddenly the children exploded on the scene, rushing out the door, their little legs carrying them forward toward the monkey bars, swings, and sliding pond. There was even a small merry-go-round powered by the push of their small legs.

Two summer school teachers, both women in their late twenties, came out behind the pack of children, moving like shepherds, their arms out over some of their wards, shouting orders and warnings: "Slow down! Don't push! Careful!"

Neil didn't recognize either of the women. Some of the children went directly to the swings or the slide, while others stood about for a few moments debating their first choice.

"They can do whatever they want?" Alpha asked softly.

"Up to a point. Long as they don't wander off or get too rowdy," Neil said.

"They look so happy," Beta said. Alpha looked at her, then back at the screaming, laughing children, most dressed in colorful summer clothing—blue and red shorts, green and white short-sleeved shirts, and pink-and-white or black-and-white sneakers and tube socks. Most of the girls had long, flowing hair. One of the boys had a sailor's cap. Even from this distance in the car, it was possible for the twins to see their cherubic faces, red with excitement and brown from hours in the sun. They all looked healthy, happy, and free.

Tania studied Alpha. At first her eyes widened with every new movement, every action. She looked quickly from one child to another, visually gobbling everything in sight. Beta sat with a soft smile painted on her face, her eyes warm, loving, feasting on the sight of other children, the first children they had really seen live.

"I guess this wasn't such a bad idea after all, huh?" Neil said softly to Tania.

She started to nod but stopped. Alpha's face was changing. Her eyes were growing smaller and the slight smile of interest and fascination was growing harder, colder. Tania focused in on what Alpha was looking at now. She had narrowed her vision intently and was staring at one little boy who had just started to pull himself up the monkey bars. The effort took all his concentration and strength.

He lifted his right leg over the bar and struggled to get his upper body up and over it as well. That accomplished, he sat down, then reached above him to the next rung. Other children, apparently at least a year or so older, were already moving over the monkey bars like small spiders, their arms and legs spinning invisible threads between the metal poles. They moved with such dexterity and speed, it looked as if they had glue on the sides of their ankles and knees.

The smaller boy stood up on the bottom rung and

reached up, pulling himself to the next rung and then the next. With each successful move, his confidence grew.

Alpha's eyes narrowed even more until they were barely slits, the blue pupils just visible. Beta knew whom she was looking at and turned to watch him, too.

"He's going to make it to the top," she said, as proud of him as she would be if she were his older sister.

"No, he's not," Alpha predicted.

Neil looked at Tania. The smile left her face.

"Neil," she said, a note of warning, an underlying vibration of fear in her voice.

"Alpha?" he said, but Alpha didn't turn from her concentrated gaze.

The little boy reached up, now two rungs from the top. His feet slid along the bar beneath him and he raised both his hands freely to take hold of the higher bar. He started to pull his body skyward, smiling at another, slightly older boy who sat on a rung to his side.

Just as the little boy lifted both his feet from the bottom rung and dangled in the air before pulling himself to the next, he screamed. The other children on the monkey bars stopped their activity and turned to him. The little boy's scream was so piercing and filled with such pain that children on the sliding pond and the nearby swings also brought their activity to a halt. The two teachers, who had been talking to one another, stopped their conversation and turned.

The little boy's hands shook violently. He seemed
unable to release his grip on the bar above him and
unable to bring his feet back to the bar below. His
entire body was set in a violent vibration. He was
unable to hold his water and a stream of urine
started down his leg.

"Jimmy!"

One of the teachers started forward, but it was
too late. The little boy's hands shot off the bar and
he fell downward, smacking his chest into the
monkey bars, then falling backward, slamming his
body on the lawn below. Other children screamed
and the teachers broke into a run.

"Oh my God," Tania said. She and Neil both
turned instantly to Alpha. She was smiling.

"Alpha," Neil said. "Did you . . ."

"Alpha, how could you?" Tania asked. She looked
at Neil.

Without hesitation, he started the engine again
and put the car into drive.

"I want to watch," Alpha said. The children had
gathered around the fallen boy who was crying
hysterically. One of the teachers held his head up
and was feeling along his shoulder and right arm.

Neil accelerated rapidly, jerking the car forward.
He made a quick turn and drove off. Both Alpha
and Beta turned to look out the rear window for as
long as they could. The last thing they saw was the
two teachers helping the fallen boy to his feet.
Alpha turned around and looked ahead, a self-
satisfied smile on her face. Tania stared at her a

moment, then looked at Beta who appeared frightened.

"Alpha, why did you do that? You did, didn't you?" Tania said. "Didn't you?" she asked in a more demanding tone. Alpha turned toward her.

"We can't climb on monkey bars, can we? We can't play on the swings or the sliding pond. We can only watch," she said, pronouncing each word sharply and deliberately. Tania turned toward Neil.

"I can't believe it," he said. "I should have considered . . . damn."

"Alpha, that was wrong. You hurt an innocent person. It's not that little boy's fault that you can't play there."

"I don't care," she said.

Tania looked to Beta, but she was obviously too frightened to say anything.

"But we took chances taking you out here. We did it because we thought it was right for you and Beta to get out of the compound and see some of the real world. You can't hurt people around you. No one will ever want to take you anywhere."

"Yes, they will," Alpha said with confidence. "Dr. Henderson will."

"Why will he?" Neil asked, remembering the real purpose to his mission.

"Because that's what he wants," she said.

"He wants you to be able to hurt other people?" Neil asked. Alpha shrugged. "To use your power to hurt other people when he tells you to? Is that it?" Neil pursued. Alpha didn't reply. *Maybe she didn't know,* he thought. "Did he tell you to use your power on Dr. Jessup?"

"Neil," Tania said in a loud whisper.

"Did he?" Neil demanded.

"No," Alpha said.

"And Mrs. Gerhart?"

"No," Alpha said.

"You did that on your own, just like you hurt that little boy just now, is that it?"

Alpha looked out the window.

"Yes," Beta offered.

"Shut up," Alpha snapped.

"I didn't like hurting the little boy," Beta said.

"I told you to shut up or I'll put you to sleep." Beta pressed her lips together instantly and looked away.

"It's not right to hurt people who don't do anything to hurt you," Tania said. "Especially people who are trying to help you. No one will want to help you if you do."

Alpha didn't reply. She stared out the window, sulking. For the remainder of the trip back to the compound, no one spoke. Beta closed her eyes and looked as if she had fallen asleep. Alpha never pulled her attention from the road outside. Both Tania and Neil stared ahead, anxious to get back and get the twins into the apartment.

There was no one around when they pulled into the parking lot. Neil backed the vehicle up to the doors, just as before, and got out. Beta opened her eyes when Tania and Neil helped to guide them out of the vehicle. Neil opened the door, looked up and down the corridor inside, then beckoned them forward.

"Just wait in here until I pull the car up to a parking spot," he said. He returned quickly and he and Tania directed the twins back through the dim corridor and up the stairs. He went out first, checked the hallway, then signaled for them to come out. It wasn't until he and Tania had them back in the apartment that he took a deep breath and relaxed. Both the twins looked exhausted now.

"Tired," Alpha said.

"Just take a nap. I'll check back with you later," he said. He and Tania watched them go into the bedroom. After they were under the blanket and had their eyes closed, Neil and Tania left the apartment and went directly to her office, neither saying anything until they had closed the door behind them.

"Well, there's no question Henderson knows what she can do," Neil said. He sat down and pulled his head back against the top of the couch. He closed his eyes for a few seconds and squeezed his temples with his forefinger and thumb. There was a dull ache in his head, the kind of ache he usually suffered when he had drunk too much wine.

"The thing is, she's mean, Neil. She's vicious. She's amoral. She knows no right or wrong. She's like some unchanneled, untamed force out there, going this way or that on the basis of a whim. I doubt that even Henderson has full control over her."

Neil nodded.

"That's why I asked if he knew about Jessup and Mrs. Gerhart."

"And yet he continues with them and lies to us. Why?"

"He's obviously doing something else with her, some kind of research. Maybe he hopes to turn her into some kind of new weapon. I don't know."

Tania thought for a moment.

"And Dr. Endermo?"

Neil didn't reply for a moment, then leaned forward.

"You know what I think is going on . . . I think one organization or department is duping and using another. It's a great cover. They locate, stage, and finance this operation under one purpose, but really run it for another. Who's to know? Henderson couldn't care less about the sociological significance of Alpha and Beta, the study of the human psyche in a crowded environment. He's here to channel Alpha's powers into something practical. I'm sure."

"We can't go to Dr. Endermo and tell him what just happened, tell him we snuck the twins out and Alpha hurt a little boy on the outside. He'd go wild and get rid of us instantly."

"I know. I hope that little boy is all right."

"Oh, Neil, what are we going to do? She manipulated us to take them out and then she did that vicious thing."

"If ever there was a bad seed . . . and the thing is it's being nurtured here under the guise of some scientific research."

"Poor Beta," Tania suddenly said. "Attached to pure evil and unable to do anything about it."

Neil nodded and sat back.

"How did this all happen?" Tania asked in the tone of a rhetorical question.

"My guess is the twins were turned over to the institute, just as Dr. Endermo explained; Henderson was brought in with the original purpose being what we originally thought. He discovered Alpha's abilities, kept them to himself, belittled whatever discoveries about her Mary Jessup and you made, snowed Dr. Endermo, and continued his own research, not caring what sort of a creature Alpha was and is becoming."

"And you were so forceful in there with him. He's not going to want you or I to go on too much longer. Somehow he'll get Endermo to let us go so he can have a freer hand and not worry about interferences from the likes of us," Tania said. "I guess I always knew something like this was happening. I sensed it, but couldn't express it or comprehend it. It was why I was so happy someone like you had been brought in."

"What still puzzles me about that is why Henderson acceded."

"He couldn't keep opposing you and maintain the cover with Endermo," Tania said. Neil nodded.

"Maybe. Or maybe somehow, someway, he's using me, too."

"How?"

"I'm not sure, but there might be a purpose to

educating the twins, especially Alpha." He looked up sharply.

"What?"

"Mainstreaming. Eventually taking them out of the secret environment and placing them in the real world so they can be of some operational value."

"But Neil, how can they put conjoined twins in the real world? They would only be looked at as freaks. No one would accept them."

"Right. As they are," he added. "But what if that were changed?"

"Changed?"

"I tell you the man's a modern day Franken-stein," Neil said.

"I don't understand," Tania said, refusing to permit herself to understand.

"We can see it ourselves . . . Beta holds her back."

"Oh, Neil, no." Tania's face softened into a face of mourning. "We've got to do something to stop it."

He nodded and sat back. His headache was getting worse. He had to close his eyes and rub his temples.

"And we've got to do it without Alpha knowing what we know and what we intend to do because there's little doubt in my mind that she would tell Henderson."

Tania nodded to herself and stood up. She walked to the window and looked out at the parking lot. She saw a limousine pull up and Dr. Endermo get out with another man.

"We've got no choice," she said softly. "We're going to have to go to Dr. Endermo."

Neil shook his head.

"Not yet. We need more. We need some concrete evidence proving what Henderson is really doing. Otherwise, we'll have the same results we had earlier."

She turned to him.

"What do you have in mind?"

"We'll have to get down into his corridor and snoop around until we find something."

"And if he finds out what we're doing?" she asked.

"We might just become part of the experiment."

"Huh? I don't understand."

"I don't think he would hesitate to turn Alpha on us like some vicious attack dog." Tania froze. "And the most frightening part of all this is we can't be sure that in some way beyond our understanding, he already hasn't."

8

Neil's session with the twins later that afternoon was very businesslike. He hid his emotions behind the work, doing what he had often accused some of his colleagues of doing, especially when it came to slower students, teaching to the rear wall. If the students between them and the wall picked up something, good. If not . . . well, the lesson was delivered.

He tried not to look at them when he spoke; he spoke in a monotone, and when he had them do some exercises in their workbook, he sat plotting the pages of text he would teach next. Occasionally, he caught a view of them in the mirror.

Alpha was just as cold to him. She concentrated on the work before her, only speaking to him when she had a question about the assignments. On the other hand, right from the moment he entered their apartment to the moment he left, Neil sensed that Beta felt ashamed. If she could express herself freely, Neil believed she would apologize for her sister's behavior. He and Tania had done something wonderful for them, and in response, Alpha had

177

nearly gotten them all in deep trouble. And why? Just because of her jealousy.

What frightened him about her was realizing how little she cared about the pain she had caused another human being. *Maybe she didn't see herself as a human being; maybe she saw herself as something alien, and therefore she had no compassion for these other creatures,* he thought. Then he realized what he was doing and pushed the thoughts from his mind. Fortunately, Alpha was concentrating on the work too much to tune in on him.

In fact, neither twin mentioned the morning's events when he came in or during their work session. It was as if it had all been a dream, a nightmare best left undisclosed. As the session wore on, he looked up and occasionally caught Alpha's confident, arrogant look. He wondered why he hadn't seen it so clearly before. Perhaps she had prevented him from noticing, or perhaps, as he had begun to suspect this morning, she was undergoing some sort of rapid metamorphosis. Studying them whenever he could, he realized the differences between her and Beta were sharper now. Even their facial features, features he had first thought were so exact it was like looking into a reflection, were different.

Alpha's nose appeared sharper, her mouth thinner. The baby fat was gone from her cheeks. Although her complexion was still rich, her skin was taut, the cheekbones more emphatic. Her forehead was wider and the creases across it were much deeper and longer.

The major change was in her eyes. She had always had a brighter, more perceptive look than Beta, but there had still been some of the same childlike softness and innocence in the blue pupils. Now they were hard and cold, moving over his face like two probes. He could almost feel the thin rays of light emanating from those orbs and piercing his skin and bones, searching his inner self with the precision of a fine X ray. He couldn't hold his eyes on her eyes long. His were like wide-open windows, exposing everything within.

He ran on and on about the math problem he was teaching, and when that was completed, moved right into the English grammar work without any sort of transition. There was no intermission, no time for idle talk as usual. Despite her remorse, Beta made no effort to interrupt the flow.

When the session was over, he gathered his materials together, told them what they should do for homework, and started out of the apartment. It was then that Alpha made some reference to the morning's events, but it was as if she had forgotten the terrible thing she had done, or, as Tania suspected, she had no sense of why it was wrong.

"Thank you for taking us on the field trip," she said. "We really enjoyed it very much."

He turned back to study her expression. There was no sarcasm, no look of irony. Beta looked down, choosing to avoid his gaze. He considered bringing up what Alpha had done to the little boy. Was it possible that she had forgotten, that such actions were immediately repressed? He decided this wasn't the time to get into it.

"You're welcome," he said. "I'll see you tomorrow."

He hurried out of the apartment, not realizing until he was in the cooler hallway that a band of sweat had broken out along his neck. There was even a trickle down the center of his chest. He took out his handkerchief and wiped his face. A moment later, Tania emerged from the observation room.

"You did the right thing," she said. "I think she was hoping you would get into it just so she could play with your mind."

"I don't think I can keep this up much longer. I'm afraid of saying or doing something that will set her off, if not against me, then against Beta. We've got to move quickly. Tonight," he said. "I'll pick you up at your place a little after eight."

"Okay," Tania replied. They had discussed a plan for getting into Dr. Henderson's office, where Neil hoped to locate some concrete evidence to present to Dr. Endermo.

After he left the institute, he called a friend of his, George Hampton, a science teacher at his school. Although George was one of the old-timers, having taught nearly thirty years, he was not one of those who had settled comfortably into a pattern, teaching the same old things year after year, relying on the same old textbooks. George subscribed to a number of science magazines and was a voracious reader. It wasn't unusual for him to make a recent scientific event the topic of his daily lesson, and he and Neil often had interesting discussions about modern technology and advances in medicine.

Fortunately for Neil, George hadn't taken himself and his family up to his cabin in Vermont yet, as he did every summer. He was home when Neil arrived and happy to see him. After a short conversation with Emily Hampton, Neil went with George into his den to speak privately. It was George who had quickly made the suggestion.

"Could see you've got something hot on your mind, buddy," he said. Just under six feet tall, George had a narrow face, its true narrowness hidden under a bushy, Hemingway-type gray beard. He wore thick, clear-plastic-framed glasses that inevitably slipped down his thin, bony nose and settled just above the small rise at the tip.

"Well, I didn't want Emily thinking I'm a bit weird coming over here to talk about extrasensory powers."

"Oh?"

"Now don't laugh, George," Neil said quickly, sitting across from him, "but one of the special ed. students under my supervision at the institute seems to have remarkable abilities."

"You mean like an idiot savant?"

"Yes, in a way. Never could understand all that."

"When it comes to the human mind, everyone's an idiot," George said, smiling. "Different parts of the brain control different functions, different abilities. An individual can have a reading disability, be slow-witted, apparently, but have an enormous talent for playing the piano." George shrugged. "What seems true is that that section of the brain that controls your ability to paint artistically or to sing or play wonderful music doesn't depend or necessarily interact with that section that controls reading comprehension or math reasoning, or even common sense behavior. It's all so departmentalized.

"Not so hard to understand," he continued as Neil knew he would. *Just get George started on something and he took it from there*, Neil thought. "If you have a neurological problem affecting the brain and your ability to see, it won't stop you from hearing, from interpreting what you feel."

"Is it possible that if one brain function is underdeveloped or never used, another might compensate by becoming stronger?"

"I've heard that blind people hear and smell better. Might be attributed to the brain making the adjustment. What exactly can this special ed. kid do?"

"Well," Neil began, concocting an event to serve his purpose. "I've seen her look down at her desk and make a pencil move. Don't laugh," he added quickly. "I've seen it."

George didn't laugh. He nodded thoughtfully.

"I've seen mentalists bend spoons. Just the other day, I was reading about some research in paraphysics involving such phenomena."

"But how? Is there a scientific explanation?"

"Of course. It involves electrical energy."

"Electrical?"

"Yep. All of us are throwing off some electrical energy, some more than others. Apparently, there are some who can generate a lot more than we would imagine. Mind you, I haven't read about anyone throwing lightning bolts across a room," George added, smiling, "but there have been some interesting studies done and some amazing findings. So what about this kid?"

"Well, it just fascinated me. What I was wondering is what would I look for to determine if it is the sort of thing you just described."

"Aside from visual observation . . . you'd need EEG readings, some neurological examinations, tests under objective, laboratory conditions to determine percentages of success to be compared with incidence of coincidence . . . why would you want to do this anyway? Don't tell me you hope to introduce this child to the world and develop her as another Amazing Kreskin or something?"

"I just wanted to prove to myself that there was nothing supernatural about it. I work with this psychologist, see . . ."

"Who thinks you're crazy. She should be more open-minded. So, I guess you're enjoying this assignment, eh?" George said, sitting back and smiling.

"Oh, yeah. And the pay's great."

"I hear you."

"George, what about thoughts?"

"Thoughts?"

"Images, mental pictures."

"What about them?"

"Do they have anything to do with this electrical energy the brain produces?"

"Sure. Thought is a chemical-electrical process. Researchers and doctors have probed the human brain with electrical impulses and stimulated memories, visions, etc. That's how we know what section of the brain controls what. And don't forget the use of electric shock treatment to subdue mental patients prone to violence."

"So if an electrical impulse could be sent into my brain, for example, it might stimulate a thought or an image . . ."

"Wait a minute," George said, with his usual quick perception. "You're not talking about opening the head and probing with an instrument, or attaching pads to your temples, are you? You're talking about sending current through the air and directing it into the mind to produce visions and thoughts." Neil nodded. George thought a moment. "Not as farfetched as people might think. I've read about work being done with radio waves transmitted into the brain. The electrical stimulation affects behavior.

"If you ask me," George said, "I think you're talking about something that could very well be the weapon of the future, an invisible weapon, transmitted great distances." He leaned forward. "Imagine beaming a current at Moscow and affecting how they behave." He sat back and nodded. "Or vice versa, imagine them beaming it at Washington."

"So you think our government is interested in such things?"

"Are you kidding? As we speak. Hey," George said, leaning forward again. "Don't go and tell any government types about your kid. They're liable to come along one night and kidnap the poor girl to put her into some laboratory somewhere."

Neil stared at George for a moment. Then he smiled.

"You're right. I'd better stop talking about this. Don't want to bring any attention to the kid. She couldn't handle it; it would be cruel."

"Teaching can be exciting sometimes, can't it?" George offered. "Kids can really surprise you. That's what I like about it, what's kept me interested all these years . . . the unpredictability factor in every classroom." George laughed. "Just when you thought it was safe to go back to the classroom," he said in a deep voice. Then he hummed the theme from *Jaws*. Neil laughed.

"Thanks for not treating me like a crackpot, George."

"Are you kidding? I'm going to miss our stimulating talks in the faculty room, buddy."

"Me, too, George. Thanks again," Neil said and stood up. He shook his friend's hand and left, a clear picture of what had to be done now taking form in his mind.

After Tania got into his car, Neil told her what he had found out about the little boy at the playground.

"I spoke to a friend of mine who teaches in the elementary school. Pretended I had heard something vaguely about it."

"And?"

"Two broken ribs," he said. "Broke 'em when he hit the bars on the way down. The kid told his teachers he got a shock from the monkey bars. First he couldn't let go and then . . ."

"Oh, God. I feel responsible, Neil."

"So do I, even though there's no longer any question in my mind that we were manipulated to a certain extent. After I left you today, I went to see a colleague of mine who teaches science. Without really telling him anything, I talked about Alpha," he added, and told her about his conversation with George Hampton, but he thought she appeared to be only half listening.

"Something else happen after I left you at the institute today?" he asked.

"Dr. Endermo stopped by," she said. "At first I thought he had found out about our taking the twins out of the compound, but that wasn't it. He wanted to know how we were doing, but especially how you were doing. He said he thought you had appeared quite high-strung and he wanted me to give him an evaluation of your mental condition. He was in the office for a good half-hour and I almost told him what we had done and what we had discovered.

"Well," she added, before Neil could chastise her. "You should have been there to hear how he was talking about Henderson. I'm sure he's not fond of the man. In fact, this was the first time I heard him so critical of Henderson. He said Henderson should have told us about Alpha's telepathic powers when it came to Beta and he should have told us about his discussion with Mary Jessup and subsequent investigations. He apologized for him and as much as called him an arrogant person. He said much of what happened could have been avoided if Henderson had been more forthcoming. I'm sure he expected I would tell you all this," she concluded.

"What did you say?"

"I told him you had a good day with the twins and you were doing what Henderson advised you to do . . . concentrating on teaching them the fundamentals. I also told him you had calmed down considerably."

"And?"

"I don't think he believed me. There was something about the way he sat there and waited. It was as if he wanted to tell me more and hoped I would encourage it by being more honest with him. But I resisted, knowing what we were about to do tonight and thinking we would be in a better position to talk with him if we found something we could show him."

"Very smart. If you told him any more, he might have confronted Henderson prematurely, put him on guard and given him another chance to explain everything away."

"That's what I was thinking."

"You're a rather bright young lady, Miss Weber,"

he said, relaxing for the first time all day. "Know that?"

"Of course. Gave myself all the tests."

He laughed, then they grew quiet as he turned onto the highway that would take them directly to Mandicott. As they drew closer, neither could avoid feeling anxious. At first that made them even quieter, sitting so still they could hear one another breathe.

"Funny how much different this place looks at night," Neil said in a loud whisper as they passed through the main gate.

The bright pole lights in the parking lot and on the roof of the buildings cast a sickly, pale tint over everything. With no one moving about, not a car started, not a door opening or closing, the structure looked positively eerie. The silence seemed to hover like some sort of dark cloud. Now, combined with the evening darkness and the long shadows cast by the lights, the stillness was even more unnerving. Neil had the feeling that at any moment, it would be shattered by a loud, piercing scream. Maybe his own.

After he pulled into a parking spot and turned off the car lights, he and Tania sat perfectly still, neither reaching for a door handle. They stared ahead, waiting to see if anyone would appear to question why they were here at this time of day. But nothing moved.

"Ready?"

Tania took a deep breath. He reached across the seat to grasp her hand and smile.

"If you don't think we should go on with this . . ."

"No," she said. "Without anything substantial, we'd be in the same position we had been in when we were in Endermo's office with Henderson . . . let's just do it and get out."

"Right."

He opened the car door. Despite his care to be relatively quiet, the sound of the handle clicking open and the moan of the car door hinges seemed to be amplified in the empty lot. It was as if the grounds came alive to alarm the inhabitants. Their footsteps echoed across the macadam. It made them walk faster until they reached the side entrance. To Neil's surprise, the door was locked.

"We should have thought of this," he said.

"We'll have to go around through the hospital proper, down through the basement, directly to Henderson's floor," Tania said.

"Hate to risk running into Endermo or Henderson or one of the others." He took a step forward to return to the car when he saw a vehicle come through the main gate and head into their section of the parking lot. Both he and Tania instinctively leaned back into the shadows. The vehicle went past them, the driver not turning their way, and pulled up to the entrance at the far end of the building.

The driver opened his door, but before he could step out, the entrance door opened and a nurse appeared, escorting a woman wearing a dark gray, ankle-length dress to the car. The nurse held the woman's arm and the woman walked with a tentative gait, like someone who had just gotten up from a sick bed.

The driver got out quickly and opened the rear door. The nurse helped the woman into the vehicle and the driver closed the door. He spoke with the nurse for a few moments, then got back into the car. The nurse returned to the entrance as the car backed up and the driver headed toward the main gate. Neil and Tania peered out from the shadows as the car went by. The driver, his face forward, still didn't see them, but the woman who had gotten into the back leaned forward and put her face to the window to look out at them as the car went by. They didn't see that much of her in the darkness, but both of them were struck by the woman's pale complexion. Neil thought he was imagining it, but the woman's eyes looked gaunt and her skin looked positively bone-white.

"Why the hell would they take a patient out that way?" Neil wondered aloud.

"I don't know," Tania said. "Maybe she wasn't a patient."

"Let's try that door. Maybe it was left open. We could go right into Henderson's area from there."

"Okay," Tania said, but she didn't sound all that determined. Neil took her hand and led her along the side of the building, remaining as close to it as he could so they would stay in the shadows. When he reached the door, he listened for sounds of anyone on the other side, then he looked back up the parking lot. Tania stared at him with anticipation. He nodded, then tried the handle.

The door opened.

Tania bit down gently on her lower lip. Neil raised his eyebrows.

"Ready?"

"Yes," she whispered, and the two of them slipped into the building very close to the stairway that led directly down to Dr. Henderson's corridor. Neil closed the door softly and without speaking, took Tania's hand again and started down the steps.

Well before they reached the lower corridor, the putrid odor of embalming fluids confronted them. It made Neil think of the jars of worms and frogs along the shelves in George Hampton's classroom. He grimaced and turned to Tania, who nodded with understanding. They didn't speak, walking as softly as they could down the shiny, immaculate steps, then hesitated at the bottom, listening.

Since most people didn't approach Henderson's area from this direction because that door to the outside was usually locked, the security guard was seated at the opposite end of the hall, facing the corridor that led back through the remainder of the institute and the hospital proper.

At this hour the lighting was even dimmer than usual because some of the corridor lights were off. There was a long section of hallway that was cloaked in thick shadows. To Neil it was as though they were standing at what was the opposite end of some tunnel. Although the guard didn't have his back to them, he was turned enough so that his immediate attention was focused on the opposite end. At this moment he was slumped back in his chair, his hands folded together on his lap. He looked like he might be sleeping.

Neil indicated they had to be as quiet as possible. Tania nodded and they started down the corridor, keeping their backs against the cold stone wall as they slid along. When they were nearly a third of the way down, a door opened two doors ahead of them on their side. The light came rushing out. They pressed their backs against the wall and waited.

The nurse whom they had seen before quickly came out of the room, wearing a light-blue cape, and closed the door behind her. It was their good fortune that she didn't look back. She turned immediately toward the other end of the corridor and headed in that direction, the click of her heels reverberating along the dark corridor.

Every sound has a sickly, hollow ring to it down here, Neil thought.

The sound of the nurse's footsteps woke the sleeping guard, who sat up quickly as she approached. She stopped and they spoke, their words an indistinct mumble evaporating in the shadows. The guard released a short, very guttural laugh in response to something she said, then the nurse continued on her way out. He watched her until she was gone, then leaned back in his chair again, folding his arms on his lap like before.

Neil and Tania did not move for a good minute. Then Neil started ahead again. With their bodies so close to the wall, they could hear any noises from within the rooms they approached. Just before they reached the door from which the nurse had emerged, they both heard the distinct sound of babies crying. Neil looked at Tania, who responded with an expression of confusion.

Neil made an impulsive decision and turned the handle of the doorway slowly until he heard the lock click open. He stood there, frozen, watching the guard to see if he had heard the sound, too. The man didn't move. Tania put her hand on his shoulder to draw him back, but he was determined to discover what was inside the room. He opened the door a few inches and peered in. The sound of the babies crying got louder. Realizing the guard would hear the amplified cries momentarily, Neil took Tania's hand and entered the room quickly with her right behind him. Then he closed the door and they confronted the sight.

They were in a small room that had a door to an adjoining room wide open. The small room was like a waiting room in a doctor's office. It was brightly lit by two long, fluorescent bulbs. There were no windows and the walls were chalk white. There was a thin, industrial quality, light-brown carpet on the floor. The room was furnished with a brown leather loveseat, a table covered with magazines beside it, and two large, cushioned, big-armed brown leather chairs across from it. There was another table between them, also covered with magazines.

"There, there," a female voice said in the other room. "Don't you two start your cryin' again."

Neil and Tania looked at one another, then moved quickly to the right side of the opened doorway. Tania could see what he wanted to do. She shook her head vigorously, but he closed and opened his eyes and nodded. Then he edged his way toward the opened, adjoining door. Tania held her breath as he leaned over so he could peer in. He gazed for a moment, then brought his body back. It took all her control not to speak, not to demand to know immediately what it was he had seen, for his face was bright red. Even his neck was flushed, and when he turned to her, his eyes were wild with amazement and fear.

9

Neil held up his hand to indicate that Tania should wait and not speak. He kept his back pressed up against the wall, and Tania did the same so they would remain out of view of whoever was talking in the next room. Whoever it was, she wasn't using tender loving care, that was certain: her tone was sharp and unsympathetic. Nevertheless, after a moment, all crying stopped. They heard what sounded like the woman placing babies into cribs, then they heard the door from that room to the hallway open and close. All was suddenly quiet.

"Neil?" Tania whispered.

He looked at her, his eyes still bright with shock.

"Wait," he said, and he peered into the adjoining room to be sure all was clear. Then, without speaking, he took her hand and led her into the room.

It was a larger, longer room, but just as brightly lit. The walls were the same chalk white, only the floor was made of a hard, shiny, cream-colored tile, instead of being covered with a rug. Like the other room, there were no windows, just an air shaft close to the ceiling. They could feel the circulation of fine, filtered air.

Tania stood beside him, her eyes now as wide, her heart beating as rapidly, and her face as flushed. Along the wall across from them were a half dozen cradles, each holding its own horror.

In the first on the far left was an infant with two heads and two necks. Both faces had their eyes closed in sleep. Both heads had a thin layer of light-brown hair, and the skin on both faces looked equally wrinkled and pink. They looked like miniaturized old women, their cheeks sunken, their skulls emphatically outlined. Their toothless mouths were slightly opened, their lavender lips turned inward.

Beside them was another set of conjoined twins, only these twins were joined lower down at the waist than were Alpha and Beta, and the twin that was mainly torso had no arms. The fuller twin had her eyes open but didn't seem to be seeing. Her lips were rather blue and her little chest was heaving with what was obviously great difficulty.

The next set of twins were joined at the temple. They slept practically at right angles from one another. They were male and looked older and stronger than the previous two sets. Their arms and legs were thicker and their torsos more swollen. One grimaced as if in pain, but the other looked contentedly asleep. Tania thought about the famous Chang and Eng. *Perhaps these twins would live as long,* she thought.

In the fourth cradle was a single infant with a

third arm growing directly out from under its right arm. The hand of this arm was clenched in a tiny fist and pressed against the infant's stomach. The hands of the other arms were open, palms upward. Other than that, this child looked normal. It was also a male.

The fifth crib contained the most hideous sight: a baby without a nose, just two openings, and only one eye and one ear; the skin was puffed into little ridges where the second eye should have been. The female infant squirmed about, but seemed incapable of making any sounds. Its little hands opened and closed and its knees jerked upward spasmodically.

The sixth crib seemed to contain a perfectly formed and normal child, but when Tania stepped farther forward to get a clearer view, she saw the baby had no legs, just two perfectly formed feet emerging from beneath its hips. The baby's complexion was sickly white, and the child's mouth was open. It was a male, but its shriveled penis looked like a grape dried on the vine. As she studied it longer, she thought it was dead. There was no movement in its chest.

Perhaps even worse than the row of cribs filled with genetically defective children was the shelf of large jars that contained either aborted or stillborn genetically defective infants. Tania turned toward it slowly, as if she were being moved against her will. Because some submerged in the formaldehyde had their eyes open, they still looked alive. These fetuses with twin heads gaped out at her with what seemed to be curious and pathetic little faces. She thought about goldfish in a bowl, and in fact, one not fully matured fetus looked more like a fish because its face was so narrow, its lips puckered and its two eyes protruded like large, gray marbles placed in the empty sockets. It appeared to have the beginnings of an extra pair of legs which would have grown out behind the primary set.

The sight of this freakish menagerie impacted on her. She felt her stomach churn and tasted the bitter acid as it rushed up her throat. She gagged and turned away. Neil put his hand on her shoulder, but she shook her head and took a step back toward the waiting room. While she worked on regaining her composure, he went to the doorway to the hall and opened it just enough to peer out.

The woman who had been in this nursery of horrors looked like the nurse whom he and Tania had seen escorting the pale-faced woman to the car that had suddenly appeared in the lot. She was standing next to the guard, who was now quite awake and rubbing his right hand along her left thigh. The two laughed. The nurse put the palm of her right hand against the guard's cheek softly and their voices became very low.

Neil looked back. Tania had her hand over her eyes and forehead and was leaning against the wall. "You all right?" he whispered. She nodded, but didn't take her hand from her face. He turned to look out at the nurse and guard again and saw that the guard had gotten up and was now following the nurse as she returned in their direction. "Damn," he said. Tania turned quickly.

"What?"

"The nurse is returning and the guard's coming with her." He thought for a moment. "Back in the waiting room. We'll slip out just as they walk back in here."

Tania hurried through the door. Neil followed and pressed his ear against the outer door to hear their footsteps as they approached. Almost too late he realized they weren't going into the nursery; they were coming directly to the waiting room. Tania sensed what was happening from the look of panic on his face; he had only to nod toward the nursery. They slipped through the adjoining doorway again just as the nurse and guard entered the waiting room.

"Wait," the guard said. Neil and Tania froze where they stood, not turning around. "I can't even stand the thought of those creatures being near me," he added.

"Oh, Phil, you're such a wimp for a man your size," the nurse replied.

"Wimp, eh?" Neil and Tania heard him push the adjoining door and saw it closing. "We'll see who's a wimp," the guard said just before the door closed. The nurse laughed. The infant with two heads in the first crib stirred with the jolt caused by the closing door, but neither pair of eyes in either head opened.

Neil and Tania heard the sounds the nurse and the guard made as they apparently settled on the settee to make love. Without any further hesitation, Neil went to the door that opened on the hallway and turned the handle slowly. He opened the door, pausing only when it threatened to squeak. He peered out first, saw the corridor was empty, then reached back to take Tania's hand and lead her out. They closed the door softly behind them.

"Let's get out of here, " she whispered.

"No. This is our best opportunity," he said, nodding back toward the waiting room where the guard was distracted with the nurse. Tania looked longingly at the closest exit to the parking lot, then followed as Neil moved quickly down the corridor to Dr. Henderson's office. He tried the door and found it was locked.

"Figures," Tania said. "Now let's go."

"Damn." Neil reluctantly started away, moving in the direction of the guard's chair and desk, where he quickly spotted the ring of keys. "Wait." He seized them and returned to Henderson's door.

"Neil, don't. It's too late."

"No, we have a little time." He tried the first three keys unsuccessfully, but the fourth opened the door. "Come on," he whispered, as he entered the office. He knew just what he was going to do about the darkness. He went directly to the X ray window on the far wall and switched on the light behind it, throwing a dull, but sufficient glow over the office. Tania waited close to the doorway, listening for any signs of the guard or the nurse while Neil rifled through the file cabinet drawers and looked through the documents.

"Neil," Tania said after what seemed to her to be a full two minutes. "We've got to get out of here before it's too late. Someone else might come along and there's no way we can explain being in this office."

"Wait . . ." He studied a folder for a moment, then took it out quickly and closed the cabinet drawer. He switched off the X ray lamp and they left Henderson's office. Neil locked the door again and returned the ring of keys to the guard's desk as they hurried by, heading for the stairway that led to an exit to the parking lot. They didn't look back. In moments they were up the steps.

They burst out the doorway. Neil took Tania's hand and they ran across the parking lot to his car. Neither said a word until Neil started the engine, backed up, and drove toward the front gate, leaving the long shadows and eerie, yellow lights behind. Tania sat back and lay her head against the top of the seat. She looked up at the roof of the car.

"Oh, God," she said. "What a horrible, horrible place. Those children, those—those monsters, and the specimens in the jars!"

"I knew it," Neil replied, staring ahead with a mad smile on his face. "I sensed it; I knew it. I felt it from the moment I met the man." He turned to Tania. "Didn't I so much as tell you?"

"But Neil, what does it mean?"

"They're collecting these grotesque birth defects

and keeping them alive as long as they can for some bizarre research Henderson is doing, I guess."

"One of them in the cribs looked dead, the one on the far right end."

"I know. They'll probably all be dead shortly. When I first read about conjoined twins, I learned that they occur once in every fifty or sixty thousand births and only about 300 live more than a few days. I imagine Henderson is doing whatever he can to prolong their lives for study."

"I guess it was just the impact of seeing so many of them at once," Tania said. "And seeing those specimens in the jars really disturbed me, because I don't think I ever had such a reaction to Alpha and Beta. I mean once I got to know them . . ."

"That's because you came into it well along the way and Dr. Endermo prepared you for it. When you first met Alpha and Beta, they had already developed personalities. You were able to develop some sort of relationship with them. Also, you were fascinated with the possibilities for your work."

"This was more like a freak show. Ugh," she said, shaking her head as if to drive out the visual memories. "Dr. Endermo must know about this, don't you think?"

"Sure."

"But probably not Henderson's real purpose."

"Well," Neil said, patting the folder beside him on the seat, "I think we might just be able to open his eyes a bit."

"Go to my place," Tania said. "It's closer and I need a stiff drink rather quickly."

Neil nodded. He checked the rearview mirror just to be sure they weren't being followed, then made a turn that would take them in the direction of her home. She sat forward, staring out the side window.

"Got a little hairy in there," Neil said, "but you were a real trooper."

She turned back to him.

"You didn't do so badly yourself. For a conservative registered Republican," she added and he laughed. It felt good to relax now, the laughter serving as a relief valve. *Little did she know,* he thought, *how frightened I had really been.* But he was proud of himself now, proud he had stuck with it. He reached across the seat and took her hand. She squeezed back and he drove on to her apartment.

She lived in a small development of town houses, each pair with dark pinewood fronts and landscaped lawns and hedges. The development was simply called PINE WOOD. Hers was the second one in on the right. A series of street lights shaped like old gas lamps illuminated the driveways. He pulled in behind her car in the car port and they got out quickly. As they made their way up the sidewalk to the stairway, he pressed the folder tightly under his arm. She took out her key and they entered the house.

He followed her through the short entryway to the living room. She snapped on a light, revealing a large, cushioned, bright-blue cotton curved sectional with two rectangular hassocks. The tables were made of a matching beechwood. She had a short driftwood lamp on each. Across from the sectional was an S-shaped lambswool chair with a dark pine pole lamp beside it. The floor was covered with a thick shag blue carpet just a shade lighter than the furniture. On the far wall were built-in light-hickory book shelves. She had two prints of Kandinsky abstracts in rich oakwood frames on the left wall. To the right was a small wet bar with a hickory wood and stone counter.

Tania threw her pocketbook down on the sectional and went right to the bar. She took out the tray of ice cubes and reached for tumblers.

"Want anything?"

"Short bourbon and soda on the rocks," he said and sat down in the center of the sectional. He took off his shoes and lay back for a moment to catch his breath, then he loosened the top buttons on his shirt and leaned forward to open the folder.

"How did you know to take that one?" she asked as she prepared the drinks.

"It has only one word on it: Alpha."

"What are we looking for?"

"Some of the things George described," he said. "And here's one . . . EEG reports." He read quickly. "There are comparisons made with Beta's EEG's." He whistled. "Some differences. He has results while they were under sedation," he continued, reporting as he perused, "results during light physical exercise and . . ."

"And what?" she asked, bringing him his drink.

"Results during telepathic communication. Look at this chart. The lines go haywire."

"We don't know how to read all this," she said, looking over his shoulder.

"No, but we can figure some of it out." He sifted through some papers. "Written reports," he announced excitedly and began reading. She kicked off her shoes and sat beside him.

"Listen to this," he said after a few minutes, "Alpha's kinetic energy increases significantly when Beta is asleep. There is no question that Beta is a drain on Alpha's paraphysical powers. Since Beta cannot be sedated without effectively sedating Alpha . . ." He read on to himself.

"What?" Tania asked when he put the papers down and looked ahead.

"I was afraid this was what he intended to do eventually," Neil said. Tania leaned forward.

"What?" she repeated.

"First, he'll perform a lobotomy on Beta. She'll become—become practically a vestigial organ drawing little or no mental energy from Alpha, whom Henderson believes can telepathically go through steel walls. And if that doesn't work, he'll try to remove her completely, amputate her at the waist in a Frankensteinlike attempt to restructure the intestines, et cetera, as best he can. Alpha won't be able to walk, but he doesn't consider that of any importance. You should read this. What a cold analysis. He can cut them up like high school students cut up worms in biology class.

"It's all here," he continued, "what his research

really is, how he wants to develop and expand Alpha's abilities until he can channel her into something lethal and do what I feared, mainstream her, get her into the world so she can be utilized."

"She's already something lethal," Tania said. "She killed two people and almost killed that child at the playground."

"Apparently that's not lethal enough for our fine doctor."

"What about those other freaky infants?"

"My guess is he's trying to locate another Alpha and another and another, or he's trying to determine what it is in the defective birth process that results in the telepathic powers." Neil paused and thought. "Sure . . . if he could duplicate the formula . . ." Neil looked at the papers again. "Wait a minute." He read on. "The women who gave birth to these creatures . . . they're described here, probably to determine if the mother's physiology has anything to do with what caused Alpha's powers." He looked up. "This one doesn't live too far away." He showed her the address.

"You think we should talk to her?"

"Why not? Maybe Dr. Endermo doesn't know how Henderson actively solicits these unfortunate mothers."

"How do you think he does it?"

He thought a minute.

"He's probably made contact with a number of maternity doctors. The women don't know. Their doctors tell them they're going to give birth to a deformed child, then Henderson probably contacts them and offers them something to go through with the birth."

"Oh, God. That sounds so revolting."

"The women are probably not very well off or . . ." He looked at the sheets. "Maybe single . . . lots of reasons why they might take his offer. They don't have to worry about the children or child." He looked up thoughtfully. "I don't think our Dr. Henderson is going to want any of this exposed and Dr. Endermo . . ."

"No one likes to be duped. All the wonderful objectives, the sociological studies, the contributions to an understanding of society and human relations . . . God, I feel like such a fool."

"Don't feel that way. Endermo is probably still forwarding your studies and findings as well as Jessup's to his superiors and you'll still have an opportunity to publish your studies. It's not a total waste of your time just because there is obviously an ulterior motive to all this."

Tania smiled.

"I bet that's just what Henderson will say."

"Got to give the devil his due." He leaned back. "We've just got to put a stop to his Frankenstein tactics. Perform a lobotomy on Beta . . ." He shook his head.

"We'll stop it," Tania said. "And we'll get Henderson far away from them."

"I hope so." He looked at his drink, then took a long sip. "Boy, am I tired all of a sudden."

"The mental tension. Gets to you faster than you think. Why don't we take a hedonistic break? Go into my whirlpool and relax."

"Just relax?" He smiled impishly.

"Whatever moves you," she said as she got up. "Excuse me while I prepare your bath, kind sir." She bowed like a geisha girl and left him smiling widely.

It's great having a psychologist for a girlfriend, he thought. *She knows just how to handle crisis and its aftermath.* He closed his eyes and waited for her to call. She had to call only once.

"Neil Richards, take that arrogant, macho man smirk off your face," Tania demanded playfully. She kissed him on the tip of his nose and, moving her body slowly from left to right, drew an imaginary line across his chest with her still firm nipples. Tania had a lean body with perky breasts that were only a shade or two lighter than the rest of her. When he pressed his lips against hers and drew her against him, she fit snugly in his arms. His body tingled every place it touched hers. Feeling her vibrant warmth and the tremble in her loins when she reached her sexual climaxes had never seemed as fulfilling as it just had.

The whirlpool had been wonderful. Naked together under the bubbling, scented water, they titillated one another with caresses and kisses until neither could hold back the wave of sexual desire. Still dripping with the warm water, they embraced on her bed and made love with a hunger and energy that threatened to consume them. His heart was still pounding.

"What smirk?"

"Oh, what smirk, he says." Tania turned over on her back and drew her hands up behind her head. She brought her knees up and gazed at the ceiling. Neil moved to his side and leaned on his left elbow so he could look right into her face, his lips inches from her cheek.

"Exactly. What smirk?"

"I can hear your male mind at work, congratulating yourself on how well you just made love to me."

"Now if ever there was a case of sexual paranoia."

"Don't deny it. Anyway . . . you should be proud of yourself. It was wonderful."

"Was it?"

"You know it was. For me, anyway. Wasn't it the same for you?" she asked, suddenly concerned. He feigned an expression of deep thought.

"Well . . ." He smiled quickly when a look of disappointment started to form on her face. "You're right, it was special."

"I know," she said, thinking.

"You do, do you? Then why did you ask?"

"Confirming my feelings. It's only natural to be pleased when your lover is as satisfied with you as you are with him."

"Always analyzing everything, huh. Well, why was it so good?"

"Why?"

"Yes, Miss Freud, why? Oh, I don't mean to suggest I don't feel very strongly about you, Tania. I'm on the verge of saying some very dramatic things and hoping you'll respond in kind, but . . ."

"But you felt a heightened sense of being. It was

more erotic than before, not that before was in any way disappointing?"

"Aptly put. So? Explain."

"Coming from danger, seeing that terror, we kind of reaffirmed our own health and life force. We weren't just having sex with one another; we were making statements. You were so forceful at times and I was so demanding." He nodded, this time really in deep thought. "Hey, don't look so worried. I promise, I won't analyze everything that happens between us, if you don't ask me to, okay?"

"Yeah, sure." He drew himself closer to her, pressing his hip against hers.

"What are you doing?"

"Trying to imagine what it would be like permanently attached to another human being."

"I would have expected you to put a different part of your anatomy against a different part of mine."

"Very funny. What are you trying to do, kill me? That would really be manslaughter."

They both laughed, then grew very quiet.

"I have to confess I've been fantasizing the same thing—being attached," she said. "There's no sense of personal identity, privacy. Neil," she said turning back to him. "Alpha can't want to see Beta removed from her. No matter how she treats her at times, she's still a principal part of her. Mary Jessup's theory was right on the money."

"Well, I didn't think she knew what Henderson has been planning for them."

"Even if he succeeded in doing it, it might just

have an effect quite opposite to what he expects. It might just make her a catatonic. In fact, I'd bet the whole pot on it. It would bring about tremendous depression, worse than the depression someone who loses an arm or a leg feels."

"I agree. Surprising that Henderson doesn't worry about that aspect. He's familiar with Jessup's papers."

"Maybe that was another reason why he wanted you there to tutor her, to fill her life with more meaning, expand her world so it involved more than Beta."

"Yeah, maybe, but I hate to think I've been part of his plan, even without knowing it."

They were both quiet for a moment.

"You never talk much about your brother," she said suddenly. "Every time we drift into conversation about our families, you brush over him quickly."

"It's still too painful. We were close. Brody and I rarely suffered from sibling rivalry. We were more like good partners, able to share, to divide responsibilities."

"I regret being an only child," she said. "Maybe that's why I'm so fascinated with Alpha and Beta. I was always jealous of and fascinated by sisters and brothers. Whenever my friends in school talked about their siblings, I would grow quiet and listen. I had all these dolls I treated like brothers and sisters."

"What stopped your parents?"

"My mother didn't want children to start with."

She turned to him. "This is painful to admit, but I later learned that my father bribed her into having me. They were living in an apartment at the time and he made a deal . . . have a baby and he'll build a house. Can you imagine my mother actually admitting to that? She told me the story herself."

"Sounds like you became a psychologist to help yourself deal with your own problems, more than to help other people deal with theirs."

"Probably right. I'm still dealing with it."

"Well, now you have an additional caseload . . . me."

"For how long?"

"What would you say to the rest of your life?"

"I deserve this," she said, nodding. "No wonderful dinner in an expensive restaurant with violins playing. No wine and candlelight, after which you would reach across the table and take my hand into yours and say, 'Tania, I love you. I can't live without you. Will you marry me?' Oh, no, instead I'm asked if I want to increase my caseload."

"All right. Strike the last few minutes. When this is over, it's right to an expensive restaurant we go."

"Doesn't have to be expensive, so long as it's cozy."

"Know just the place. Well, it's more like a diner."

"Neil Richards."

He laughed and looked at his watch.

"I'd rather you didn't go home tonight," she said softly. "I'd just feel better knowing you were right beside me." She didn't have to explain why. The ugly images were still flashing across his consciousness also.

"Okay. Tomorrow's a day off. After breakfast, we'll take a ride and see if we can talk to that mother who lives near here. See if we can find out how these women are brought into Henderson's project and if they know anything about it at all."

"Doubt that they do."

"Nevertheless, maybe we'll have one person whom Endermo can talk to, if need be."

"What if she calls Henderson right after we see her?"

"We'll make an immediate appointment with Dr. Endermo. It will be too late for him to stop us."

She nodded.

"There was one in one of those jars," she said, "with its mouth open. It looked like it died screaming."

"I know what you mean. I tried not to look at those specimens."

She rubbed up against him and they kissed. Then she closed her eyes. Almost immediately, she opened them again.

"Neil."

"Yes?"

"I just thought of something. Remember how Alpha always used to ask about the others, how she even asked you the first time you went in there?"

"Yeah."

"She knew; she always knew. She was trying to tell me, but I wouldn't listen, wouldn't consider such an idea."

"Yeah."

"It makes you wonder, doesn't it?"

"What do you mean?"

"How much about all this she really does know. Maybe—maybe she knows more than even Henderson thinks."

"Maybe," he said, and they both fell asleep wondering.

10

The woman's name was Patricia Hooks. She lived in Otisburg, a hamlet and township fifteen miles southeast of Centerville. Neil knew the area and described it as primarily farm country. Once they left the major intrastate highway, they had to drive much slower because the road was narrow and full of curves. Twice they found themselves behind farm tractors and had to go along at fifteen miles per hour until the road opened up sufficiently for them to chance passing the vehicle. The driver of the second tractor, a sullen looking man in coveralls, stared ahead like a man fixed on a dream. Unlike the first farmer, he made no effort to pull aside so they could get by easily.

"Thinks the road is part of his farm, I guess," Neil commented when they went by. "I've met some of the people from this area. They're stiff-necked, nineteenth century."

Most of the farms they passed were well kept. The houses looked freshly painted; some actually glittered in the warm, bright sunlight. It was obvious the people took pride in their property;

lawns and gardens showed tender loving care. They passed a beautiful horse ranch, a training farm for trotters. It was picturesque with its track, bright white fences, and long, sprawling, modern ranch-style house. A trainer and driver worked with a dark brown horse on the track while colts looked up from the grazing fields and gazed with lazy eyes as he and Tania drove by.

Here and there they passed smaller homes, two-story wooden structures with screened-in front porches, turn-of-the-century architecture charac-terized by Queen Anne roofs, hand-carved wooden eaves, and eyebrow attic windows. Elderly men and women sitting in rocking chairs or lounging on settees looked aloof and only vaguely interested in their passing vehicle.

"You do feel as if you've turned back time when you get off the highway and head down here," Tania replied. She gazed up periodically from the folder. She had been studying the chart on Patricia Hooks, trying to determine what she could about the woman before they met her.

They had decided they would pretend to be members of Dr. Henderson's personal staff, visiting her as part of a follow-up. Hopefully, because they knew so many details about her delivery, she would buy the cover and talk freely.

From the chart they knew that Patricia was only twenty-three years old, five-feet six-inches tall and 120 pounds. Beside facts about her physiology, blood type, etc., there was a brief description of her mental capacities: I.Q. scores, Rorschach results with personality profiles, TAPs, and vocational aptitude analyses.

She was a woman of average intelligence with a proficiency for abstract reasoning, undeveloped as it was. The only work she had ever done was menial. She had been brought up on a chicken farm and spent a good deal of her youth candling and packing eggs. For a short period, she had worked as a waitress in a nearby diner.

They knew she had been married, but her husband had apparently deserted her. She already had two children, a boy, age five; a girl, age three. From the statistical data, Tania concluded she had been pregnant and delivered her first child nearly two years before she had gotten married. There was a strong suggestion that the father of the first child was not the father of the second.

"Considering when her husband supposedly deserted her, it's safe to assume that the third pregnancy was definitely not a result of intercourse with him," Tania told Neil.

"So she sleeps around. A deserted woman with two children . . . ideal subject for Henderson. Any offer of money would have been appealing."

"There's no mention here of any obstetrician," Tania said.

"Henderson probably made an agreement to keep the names of cooperating doctors off any records."

Her address turned out to be on an unpaved side road. Neil stopped, confirmed the road sign, and turned onto the gravel and sand street. Eventually, they found a mailbox with the name HOOKS on it and saw that she lived in a trailer, still set on its original wheels, about fifty yards off the road.

It was an old, worn looking house trailer that Neil thought was probably from the sixties. The brown and white aluminum exterior was streaked and rusted. There was a set of four wooden steps leading up to the main entrance; a rear entrance had no steps and looked unused. A television antenna protruded from the top of the trailer, but leaned threateningly to the right.

The small patch of lawn in front of and to the side of the trailer was filled with bald spots. The grass looked trampled, rather than cut, even though there was a one-and-a-half horsepower push mower lying against the south end of the trailer. A faded red tricycle was toppled on its side in front of the trailer and there were toys scattered all about. A dirt driveway that looked cut out of the earth with one or two passes from a bulldozer led up to the north end of the trailer. Parked there was a 1980 burgundy Ford Mustang, the rear end badly dented. Beside it lay a pair of used snow tires.

"I can't imagine our Dr. Henderson coming up here," Tania said.

"I can. Think of the anonymity. This woman looks about as lost and forgotten as anyone could be. Lives off welfare, most likely disowned by any of her relatives. No one really cares what happens to such people."

"I wonder how much they gave her."

"Didn't have to be much. Whatever it was, it looked big to her, that's for sure."

He turned up the driveway and stopped right behind the Mustang. Almost immediately, the five-year-old boy opened the door and peered out. He was dressed in a stained T-shirt and a pair of cut-off jeans. He was barefoot and his untrimmed, dark brown hair was falling over his forehead and down his temples. He stared out with big, curious, hazel eyes, his face tanned from hours and hours of being left on his own to play in the sun. A moment later, the three-year-old girl, naked from the waist up and wearing only a pair of what were once light-blue-and-white shorts, but were now mostly egg shell with the blue tint nearly gone, came up beside him. Her unbrushed strawberry-blond hair was long, and her face was smeared with peanut butter and jelly. She held the remnant of her sandwich in her left hand.

Neil smiled and got out of the car. He heard Patricia Hooks say something indistinct and almost instantly, the little boy slammed the door shut, nearly catching his little sister in between the door and the jamb. Tania got out slowly and came around the car.

"Tobacco Road if I ever saw it," she said, looking about.

Neil nodded.

"I imagine she's some sort of an embarrassment to the old-timers here, a blight on the landscape."

"Ready?"

"I'm right behind you," Neil joked. They walked up the short steps and rapped on the metal door. The little girl started to cry within and they heard

Patricia Hooks snap at her. She had a deep, nasal voice. The girl's crying became a soft whimper almost immediately. A moment later, Patricia opened the door.

She was dressed in a sheer pink-and-brown housecoat and had her reddish-brown hair up in hot rollers. She had a cigarette in her right hand, the long ash at the end threatening to fall. She was a pale-skinned woman with light freckles along her forehead and temples. Neil imagined that for a short time in her life, she had had a soft, cute face because her features were small and well-proportioned in relation to each other. Now, her teeth were brown and her eyes held the tired, worn look of a woman nearly twice her age.

She was very thin, perhaps ten or so pounds less than she was described to be on the chart. Her emphatic collarbone was well exposed because she had the first third of her housecoat buttons undone. There was a burst of carrot-colored freckles just above her cleavage; she was wearing a bra that looked frayed and worn at the edges. Neil could see that at one time she had a perky little figure. She reminded him of junior high girls who developed rapidly, but whose bodies began to take on a matronly look when they reached Patricia's age. It was as if the process of maturation was sped up throughout their lives.

"What'd'ya want?" she demanded.

"Are you Patricia Hooks?" Tania asked in a congenial tone. Patricia's eyes narrowed and her gaze moved from Tania's feet to her head quickly. Then she looked suspiciously at Neil.

"So?"

"We're with Dr. Henderson," Tania said, maintaining her smile. She widened it when she looked down at the little girl who stood close to Patricia, hanging on the skirt of her housecoat and keeping her thumb in her mouth. The little boy sat on the couch to the right and stared.

To the left was the kitchen area, the small table still covered with dishes and glasses, a loaf of white bread, an opened jar of jelly and one of peanut butter. The living room area on the right consisted of only a couch, a small rectangular table, and a wooden chair with rust-tinted cushions. The linoleum on the floors was worn and even ripped up in spots. The curtains that hung limply over the windows looked like the original ones, never taken down to be washed and ironed. The walls of the trailer were made of a cheap, pasteboard paneling, much of it streaked or dented and some of it peeling.

"What'd'ya want?" Patricia asked again, this time straightening her back and arching her neck suspiciously.

"Well, we're part of Dr. Henderson's team and our assignment is to do follow-ups."

Patricia did not back up. She eyed Neil again.

"What the hell does that mean?" she finally responded.

"We're here to see how you're getting along since

the delivery. It's very important to our project," Tania said.

"Do I get any more money for it?"

Tania looked at Neil.

"We'll pay you twenty dollars an hour," he said, "even if we don't take up an hour."

"What do I gotta do?"

"Just answer some questions," Tania said. "Nothing more."

Patricia considered a moment, then backed up to let them enter.

"Billy, get the hell off the couch and let them sit down," she snapped. "Go on outside and play with Melanie. Go on."

The little boy moved obediently. He took his sister's hand, and without taking his eyes off Neil and Tania, went through the doorway.

Patricia took some magazines off the couch and waited.

"Thank you," Tania said. She and Neil went to the couch. Patricia sat in the chair and stuffed her cigarette into an ashtray on the small, wobbly, matching table.

Tania took her attaché case off her shoulder and unzipped it. Patricia watched her every move intently. Tania then took out a notebook and pen and sat back, smiling.

"My name is Brenda Gerson and this is Dr. Fields," she said.

"What kind of doctor?" Patricia asked quickly.

"A psychologist," Neil said. "Clinical," he added.

"You wanna know if I gone crazy since the birth, is that it?"

"No," Neil said smiling. "Not at all. Although I can imagine how you must have felt afterward."

"Why's that?"

"Well, considering . . ."

"That's part of what we want to know," Tania said quickly. "How did you feel afterward?"

"Very tired. They shoulda give me more time to rest in the hospital. And they promised me some help with the kids and I never got it," she said angrily. Her eyes brightened and she pulled the corners of her mouth up. Instantly, Neil felt sorry for her children. He had seen too many cases just like this when he taught at the public school: children living with a single, sullen parent who resented the responsibility. Alone, they turned their frustrations on their children who then became withdrawn.

"Uh huh, but you did get paid," Neil said, a little sharper than he intended.

"I shoulda gotten more."

"How much more did you think you should have gotten?" Tania asked. Patricia thought a moment, then shrugged.

"At least another five hundred dollars. Especially because of how they treated me afterward."

"How did they treat you?" Neil asked.

"Don't you know?"

"Well, we weren't with you. We're part of the team who meets with people sometime later, so . . ."

"They weren't very nice," Patricia said. "Gettin' me outa there like that and not tellin' me anythin' about the kids. Was they boys, girls, what?"

"You mean," Tania said, dropping her professional tone for a moment, "you never saw the children you gave birth to?"

"How could I see them through that sheet?"

"Sheet?"

"I thought you said you was part of Dr. Henderson's staff," Patricia said and pressed her clenched fists against her thighs to straighten her torso even more.

"We told you," Neil said. "We're only part of the staff that comes in afterward. What sheet?"

"The sheet. The sheet." They stared at her. She leaned forward, smirking. "They hung this stupid sheet from the ceiling and wheeled me into it until it was up to my waist. Then they did the birthin' and I heard the kids cryin', but when I asked what they was, the nurse said, 'What do I care?'"

Neither Neil nor Tania said anything for a moment.

"So?" she asked. "What was it?"

"It was . . . twins, boys," Neil said quickly.

"Figured it was twins." She nodded, smiling because she was proven correct. "Dr. Henderson told me I didn't have twins goin', but I keep tellin' him it feels like twins. I knew what it would feel like, havin' already had two children," she added, gesturing toward the doorway to indicate Billy and Melanie.

"Imagine you would. Probably he didn't want to alarm you," Neil said.

"Oh, yeah. That's not what I think," she said. She leaned forward, her face screwed tightly into an intense look of anger. "He probably didn't want to give me another five hundred bucks. Probably thought if I knew there was another child, I would ask for another five hundred. Only paid me for one. Said there'd be only one. You tell him I want my extra five hundred now.

"Well, it's only fair," she continued, sitting back again. "I was carryin' two of his instead of one and all that time . . ."

"Of his?" Tania said. She smiled and shook her head. "You mean because he paid you in advance, you called the baby his?"

"Huh?" Patricia stared at both of them a moment, her eyes getting narrow again. "Say, are you sure you're with Dr. Henderson?"

"Of course," Neil said.

"Well, how come you're askin' me that, then?"

"We're confused," Tania said quickly. She looked at her notebook. "You're Patricia Hooks and we were told that after your own doctor . . ."

"My own doctor?" Patricia stood up. "Say, what the hell is this? I didn't have no doctor of my own."

Both Neil and Tania felt they were losing it quickly. It was time for a quick performance.

"I told you," Neil said to Tania. "I told you they were sending us out with only half the information so we wouldn't make any preliminary judgments."

"Well, that's part of any objective case study," Tania responded, improvising just as quickly.

Patricia looked from one to the other as they continued.

"Yes, but the preliminary data in this case is not going to affect the conclusions. You take the APT tests that were run on Mrs. Hooks and then you punch in the subsequent Rorschach . . ."

"That's just it," Tania said continuing the gibberish. "I don't think there was a subsequent Rorschach."

"Was there?" Neil asked turning back to Patricia.

"Huh?"

"Listen, this isn't your fault. We were sent out with incomplete data and asked to run an update. Now you say you had no personal physician who recommended you to Dr. Henderson when you discovered you were pregnant and the child was malformed."

"Malformed?"

She sat down again.

"Well, how did you get into the program?" Tania asked. "I'm sorry," she added when Patricia did not respond. "We have some wrong information and the data sheets are obviously screwed up. This trip is going to be a total waste."

"You mean you won't give me the twenty?"

"Oh no," Neil said, taking out a twenty. "Here."

Patricia leaned forward and took it quickly.

"I still should get the extra five hundred. He told me it was only one child. That's all he was supposed to have put in."

"Put in?" Neil said.

Tania touched his arm to indicate they should go slowly with Patricia.

"You mean, that's what he told you when he asked you to be a surrogate mother," Tania stated as if translating.

"Yeah, that was it. He called me a surrogate. I remember that word because I seen this woman on television the other day. She was tryin' to get a baby back. And you know what? They give her ten thousand dollars to be a surrogate. He gave me only five hundred. I was goin' to call and complain 'bout it." She took another cigarette from the pack in the pocket of her housecoat. "I did call," she confessed, "but they acted like they never heard a me. I didn't want to carry on about it, so I hung up."

She stuffed the twenty into her other pocket and lit her cigarette. Neil and Tania simply stared at her.

"He should have given you more," Tania said. "I'm going to talk to him about it."

"Will ya?"

"Definitely. It's unfair. They brought you to the hospital and inserted a fertilized egg into your womb. You carried the pregnancy to term, then delivered the offspring without ever knowing what it was," Tania summarized, more for her and Neil's benefit than for Patricia's. "Then they released you from the hospital too early and left you on your own, more or less."

"A nurse came by here once or twice," Patricia admitted, "to give me some medicine, but no one helped with the children," she added quickly. "And they promised that."

"Unfair," Tania said. "All right. There is someone we should speak to. He's the head of the hospital and he doesn't know how unfairly you've been treated. Would you be willing to go with us to the hospital later today or tomorrow and tell him what was done to you? He's got to know how badly run this program is. And I'm sure he'll see to it that you are fairly compensated."

"You mean they'll give me more money?"

"I believe so."

"Maybe as much as that woman on television got? She gave birth to only one and they gave her ten thousand," Patricia added quickly.

"You'll have to tell him that."

Patricia considered.

"All right. I'll do it," she said. "When?"

"Let us go back and talk to the head doctor, then we'll contact you. What's your telephone number?"

"555–3464."

Tania wrote it down and then nodded to Neil. He and Tania stood up.

"Don't worry," Tania said. "We're going to see that the right things are done here."

"I ain't worried," Patricia said. "But I should get what's mine for doin' what I did."

"Definitely."

They went to the door.

"We'll be in touch," Neil said. "Very soon."

They walked out. The two children, seated on the

grass, looked up at them as soon as they emerged from the trailer.

"Billy, get the hell off the cold, wet ground with your sister, damn it!" Patricia commanded from the doorway. The little boy and girl stood up. Tania smiled at them, then she and Neil went directly to the car and got in. Patricia remained in the doorway to watch them back out. Tania waved as they turned around and headed away, but Patricia simply watched them go.

"What do you think all this means?" Neil asked as soon as Patricia Hooks's mailbox was out of view. He was making his own conclusions rapidly, but he wanted to hear Tania say it first.

"All along we thought Henderson was gathering birth defects and keeping them alive for his experimentation. That was horrible enough. But here he is, genetically engineering double monsters to work on some theory he has developed concerning extra-sensory powers."

"He pays these poor women five hundred dollars, fertilizes one of their eggs with genetically altered sperm or alters the eggs first, then implants these genetically manipulated fertilized eggs into the womb of the unsuspecting mother, telling her she's serving as a surrogate for some couple unable to have children."

"He keeps their offspring a secret from them, pays them off and gets rid of them as quickly as possible," Tania concluded.

"I was too kind when I called him a Frankenstein.

Can you imagine, that menagerie of horror back there in the institute is all his creating."

"Do you think he created Alpha and Beta?" Tania wondered aloud.

"My guess is no. It think this all might have started with the primary purpose being what we thought. Then Henderson was brought into it, discovered things about Alpha and began to formulate his theories. He was probably working in the field anyway."

"Of course he was. I told you, he's one of the foremost authorities on genetics. Now what do we do?"

"Just what we planned. Call Endermo. Show him the folder and make arrangements for him to meet the Hooks woman. He'll bring it to an end."

"When you think about it, what an ingenious way Henderson went about this . . . using one government project as a cover for a covert one that would nauseate most people. Me, you, even Dr. Endermo, are all window dressing."

Neil grew thoughtful. Unlike during their trip to Patricia Hooks's trailer, he barely noticed any scenery at all. As soon as he turned onto the intrastate highway, he accelerated, determined to get them to the institute and Dr. Endermo as fast as he could.

"By now Henderson must have discovered his folder is missing," Tania conjectured. "Since we were the ones who brought Alpha's powers to Endermo's attention and forced that meeting, he surely suspects us, don't you think?"

"Yes." He thought for a moment, then turned to

her. She was actually frightened by the expression on his face.

"What?"

"Suppose Henderson does have strong control over Alpha. He's sure to turn her against us. That could even have been what happened to Mary Jessup. She found out too much and Henderson gave orders."

"But what about Mrs. Gerhart? She was just a cook; and you saw what Alpha did to that little boy and why. She's just malicious."

"Maybe. Or maybe she learned the extent of her power from Henderson and went a bit wild. She's a wild card, unpredictable, but that doesn't mean he can't use her when he wants to."

"All right," Tania said. "We'll stay away from the twins until we speak to Endermo and get him to act."

"Wait," Neil said after he parked the car and they got out. "Let's not enter the institute the way we always do. I just want to be extra careful about everything until we get to Dr. Endermo."

Tania looked at the side entrance they always took. Neil's paranoia was infectious. Normally benign objects like door handles suddenly looked threatening. Surely Henderson anticipated their going to Dr. Endermo with the folder. He would do all he could to prevent their meeting.

"Maybe we should call him and have him come out of the institute," she said without taking a step farther.

"He might not come at all, or he might not come

for some time. He'll want to know why and this isn't the kind of thing we can explain over the phone. No, I think we'll be all right if we just go directly to his office." He inhaled deeply, looking like a man about to run a marathon. "I hope," he muttered under his breath. Tania heard that and held back. He took her hand and they moved toward the front entrance of the institute.

The lobby looked a little busier than usual; there were two extra security guards on duty. He and Tania sensed a frenzied atmosphere, but they didn't stop to speak to anyone.

"Here," Neil said, handing Tania the folder. "Put this in your briefcase so it's not easily visible until we get into Dr. Endermo's office."

She took it quickly, inserted it, and zipped her briefcase closed, then they continued down the hallway toward the turn that would take them into the research institute. The main corridor was as deserted and quiet as usual.

"My heart's pounding," Tania whispered. The way she slowed down a step as they reached each doorway reminded Neil of the way Dr. Endermo walked through the corridor the first day he had come to visit. *Perhaps he instinctively sensed danger from the very start*, Neil thought.

"Mine isn't exactly in a pleasant, syncopating rhythm." He tried smiling.

They both stopped dead in their tracks when they heard a door open down the corridor. They watched as one of the maintenance men who had clearance for this section emerged pushing a pail of water on wheels and a mop. He turned a corner and disappeared. Tania and Neil looked at one another, then went directly to Dr. Endermo's door.

There was no one in his outer office. His secretary was not behind her desk. Neil could see, however, by looking at the phone on the desk that someone in Dr. Endermo's inner office was speaking on one of the lines. He didn't hesitate; he went to the door and knocked. Then he looked at Tania and opened the door without waiting for any invitation.

They both stepped in together and stopped, their instant reaction identical—eyes wide, mouths agape.

Dr. Henderson sat behind Dr. Endermo's desk.

"I'll speak to you later about it," he said into the phone, then he cradled the receiver and looked up at them.

"News travels fast, even in this section," Henderson said, smirking. He sat back and shook his head. "You were both off today, right?"

"News?" Neil looked around. "Where's Dr. Endermo?"

"Oh? So you don't know," Henderson replied. He sat forward, a look of curiosity on his face now. "You mean you just stopped by?"

"Know? Know what?" Tania demanded.

"It seems certain now that Dr. Endermo suffered a coronary. He's in CCU," Henderson said.

"Oh no," Tania said.

"I kept advising him to go in for some tests. He had a persistent circulation problem. Told me his arm kept falling asleep; it felt like little electric shocks running up and down it. But what's that saying about the shoemaker without shoes?"

"How bad is he?" Neil asked.

"Bad enough. For the time being, I will handle his responsibilities, so if you two had a problem . . ."

"It's nothing that can't wait," Neil replied quickly.

"It might be a long wait," Henderson said. He smiled that coldly calculating smile that gave Neil the chills.

Neither he nor Tania replied. They turned and left the office and without speaking, headed quickly for the front entrance.

11

"I can't believe how I was shaking in there," Tania said. "Do you think he saw how I was shaking?"

Neil opened the front door for her and she stepped out of the hospital lobby. Both had felt constrained to speak until they were out of the research institute. The sun, now on its westward slide, seemed pasted against the sea blue sky. It looked like a hot, orange wafer desperately avoided by the small puffs of clouds hooked on an eastward wind. Two interns and a nurse hurried up the steps before them, all laughing in chorus to some joke. Neil didn't respond to Tania until the three went by and entered the hospital.

"He looked so damn confident, so assured of his control. I felt like leaping over the desk and wringing his neck." He stopped on the sidewalk and looked back at the hospital, then at the parking lot as if undecided as to which direction he should go.

"He knew we had taken the folder; he knew we were going to take it to Endermo. Surely he must have turned Alpha on the man."

"That whole business about electric shocks up and down his arm . . . that was for our benefit so we would know how it happened and what could happen to us if we crossed him. I'm sure of it," Neil said. "Come on." He took her arm and started toward the car.

"Where are we going?"

"I don't know. Away from here. Someplace we can think without fear that our thoughts might be manipulated."

"We'll go back to my apartment," she said. She hugged herself when they reached the car. "God, I'm still shaking." He opened the door for her.

"You'll feel better when we're out of here."

She got into the car quickly and they drove off.

Back at her townhouse, she made them both a drink. Like a parrot, she kept asking herself as well as him, "What do we do?" He sat thinking, various emotions passing through him simultaneously. He was sullen and angry, fearful and anxious. He hated the frustration. She saw the turmoil in his face when she sat across from him after giving him his drink. For a while they were both quiet, both still feeling the aftershock. Then, he suddenly reached across the couch and seized her briefcase. Because he moved so forcefully and unexpectedly, she actually jumped in her seat. He unzipped the briefcase and took out the folder.

"What are you looking for?" she asked. He didn't reply. He rifled through the papers until he found one and reread it while she waited impatiently. Finally, he looked up.

"I thought I remembered this." He held out the page, but he didn't wait for her to read it. "Henderson reports to somebody, somebody higher up. There's a telephone number and reference code," he added, pointing them out on the page. "I don't know; it might just be a bookkeeper, but if his higher-ups realized he screwed up and might bring embarrassment to them . . ."

"Embarrassment?"

"What if we turn all this over to the newspapers? Sure," he added, anticipating her response, "I know they'll think we're crazy at first, but we'll bring the reporter to Patricia Hooks and he'll hear her tale. Television and radio are sure to pick it up. It could be a big enough splash to bring the experiment to an end."

"I don't know. Newspapers? Television?"

"You heard Endermo go on and on, time in and time out, how important it was not to let any of this out to the public."

"But he wanted only to protect the twins."

"Exactly, and that's what we will be doing if we do let it out. Ironic, but true."

"It's going to be a circus," she said. "Can you imagine pictures of Alpha and Beta on the six o'clock news?"

"Well, maybe we won't have to actually do it. Maybe if I call this number and speak to NX31, whoever that is, and tell him all we know and what we intend to do . . . maybe Henderson will be out on his ear within the hour. After all, he really did screw up. They might not even know about the deaths of Mary Jessup and Mrs. Gerhart, and now Dr. Endermo . . . I'm going to do it," he said impulsively. He stood up. She looked at him a moment, then nodded.

"Okay. There's not much else I can think of at this point anyway, and I know I don't want to go back to that place with Henderson at the helm and Alpha at his beck and call. She doesn't know what she's doing, but that doesn't make it any less lethal or make her any less dangerous to us."

"Exactly. This is a New Jersey number," he said, moving to the phone. He dialed and waited. She came over to stand beside him as he spoke. Wherever it was, the receptionist greeted him by simply repeating the phone number. "I want to speak with NX31," he said. There was a pause, then he heard her ringing through. "She's ringing," he whispered. A man came on.

"NX31."

"I'm with Henderson," Neil said quickly. He waited, but the man said nothing. "There has been a foul-up at Mandicott."

"Who is this, please?"

"It doesn't matter. I'm the man with Dr. Henderson's folder on the twins," he said. "Alpha has killed two people and may have killed a third. She's out of control. Henderson has lost it. Everything must be terminated immediately."

"Can I have your reference number?" the voice requested in a mechanical tone.

"There is no reference number. I am not working for you. I'm working for the twins." He waited for a response to that piece of information, but there was none. "If Henderson's project isn't packed up and out of the hospital by the end of the day, the folder will be turned over to the media. Do you understand?" After a pause, there was a response.

"Where can you be reached?"

"I can't be reached," Neil said. "By the end of the day today," he repeated. "I mean it," he said, and cradled the receiver quickly. "There," Neil said. "Let's see if that doesn't wipe that arrogant smile off Henderson's face, eh?"

"Whom did you speak to? What did he say?" Tania asked.

"I don't know. Some voice." He looked about nervously. Then he went to his drink and took a long swallow. "He wanted my reference number and when I told him I worked for the twins and not for Henderson, there was dead silence."

"Why did you say you couldn't be reached?"

"I imagine he wanted to know where I was so maybe they could send someone to talk us out of it."

"But Henderson will tell them who we are."

"He's not going to be happy telling anyone anything. He'll mostly have explaining to do, I'm sure. What we'll do is go back to the institute, park, and remain in the car. We'll see what happens . . . whether Henderson leaves or not and packs up his project."

"He can't do all that in one afternoon, Neil."

"He can start. It's not our problem now; it's his. Or theirs, whoever they are. Jesus," he said, feeling his forehead. "I'm drenched. I think I'll take a quick shower. We want a little time to pass before we return to the institute anyway."

"Not a bad idea."

"You want to go first or should we go together?"

"I'm too nervous to be sexy," she said.

"Right. You go first. I'll finish my drink and peruse the folder one more time, just in case I missed anything else we might be able to use."

He hugged her. For a moment it seemed as though she wasn't going to let go.

"I just wish we had someone powerful on our side, someone we could trust."

"We'll be all right, and so will the twins—once this madness is brought to an end."

"Right." She smiled, then started for the shower. "I'll be fast."

"We've got time. Don't rush."

He returned to the living room to read and became so absorbed in it that he didn't realize when she returned.

"Your turn," she said.

He looked up. Her hair was freshly brushed and she was wearing a blue, cotton short-sleeved blouse and a pair of stone washed jeans.

Even at the height of this crisis, he thought, *she looks so bright and delicious.*

"You were right about the shower. I feel energized."

"You look great."

"My work clothes. I figured that . . ."

The phone rang, its sound suddenly so piercing,

so ominous. Neither moved until it rang again. She went to it quickly.

"Hello. Yes, this is she."

Neil rose from the couch and walked up beside her when she gestured for him to do so.

"Yes," she said and listened for nearly a minute. "I see. Of course. No, I . . . one moment, please." She pressed her palm against the mouth piece. "It's a nurse from CCU at Mandicott. She said Dr. Endermo asked to see us. She said he has improved some and the doctors feel that we can come up, that he is so intense about seeing us, it would help calm him and help his condition if we went up, but we have to go right away. What should I tell her?"

"He must have realized what we were telling him was true and now understands what happened to him. We'll go, of course. He can still help, by telling us whom to see and where to go. That's probably why he wants to see us."

"Maybe you're right. Yes," Tania said to the nurse. "Tell him we're on our way. 'Bye." She cradled the receiver.

"Let's get going," Neil said and started for the door with her. "Wait." He turned back. "I'll bring the folder to prove what Henderson's been doing," he said, and returned to the living room to retrieve it. Then they were on their way.

They parked in the hospital visitor's lot at Mandicott and went directly to the reception desk. The woman at the desk was part of a local charity work organization known as The Pink Ladies. Dressed in pink aprons and bodices, they assisted nurses, ran the hospital gift and book shops, and manned the front desk. Neil thought he recognized the woman, who, it turned out, was the mother of a student he had had two years ago, Peter Boxner.

"Mr. Richards. I was wondering if the name on this pass was the same Mr. Richards. Someone told me you were working here. What do you do here?"

"Oh, it's a long story," he said and smiled. "I'm in a bit of a rush, otherwise I would go into it."

"Maybe on the way out," she replied and handed him their passes to CCU. She exchanged a smile with Tania.

"I remember that woman now," Neil said as they headed for the elevator. "Mother of one of my students. Whenever she came for a parent conference, she was more interested in what was going on with some of the other students than with her son. You can be sure she's going to do everything possible to find out what she can about us."

"Maybe we should bring her along," Tania joked.

The elevator took them to the fifth floor; CCU took up the entire west end. They passed through the double doors and approached the nurse's desk at the center of the large room. One nurse sat before a row of monitors. Another attended some patients and a third stood waiting for them behind the counter.

Three beds to their immediate left were occupied by elderly people, two men and a woman; there was a young man on their right. Looking across the room and to the right, they saw a private room with large front windows. The CCU nurse behind the counter indicated that was where Dr. Endermo was.

"He's doing a lot better," she explained. "He might even be moved to Step Down tomorrow."

"That's great," Tania said. The nurse escorted them to the doorway. Sanford Endermo looked up from the bed. The EKG monitor beeped and the numbers jumped as he adjusted himself to sit up. The nurse moved forward quickly and arranged his pillows. The tall man looked very uncomfortable in the hospital bed. His long feet poked up and into the white blanket so emphatically it looked as though his toes might pop through any moment. His hair hung limply over his forehead and temples, yet he managed a smile as soon as they came through the doorway.

"Now you take it easy," the nurse commanded. "I'll be watching your monitor," she warned.

"I understand, Lucy. Don't worry. I'm calm now."

The nurse maintained her stern expression as she left the room.

"Well, here we are," Endermo said. "Don't be afraid. Come closer."

"How do you really feel?" Tania asked, stepping forward. She thought he had good color.

"About two thousand percent better. It really hit me when it hit me. I could almost see the lightning bolt come through the door," he added. Neil, who stepped up beside Tania, nodded knowingly.

"You know why and you know how now, don't you?" he asked. Endermo nodded and looked toward the doorway to be sure no one else was in listening range.

"I should have paid more attention to you two. It was just that your stories sounded so farfetched at the time. I couldn't give them credence, not in the face of the evidence Dr. Henderson was presenting. I'm sorry, for myself as much as for you now," he added. "And especially sorry for the twins. What's that biblical expression—'They know not what they do.'"

"As long as you'll be all right," Tania said.

"But that wasn't the case for poor Mary Jessup and poor Mrs. Gerhart," Endermo quickly replied. He looked up at them, with widened, inquisitive eyes. "Am I right?"

"I think it's all here," Neil said, bringing the folder out from under his arm.

"What is that?"

"We had better start at the beginning," Tania said to Neil. He nodded and brought a chair up close to the bed for her, then got one for himself. "First, we have to tell you that for all sorts of reasons, not the least of which was Alpha's own desire and firm control of our energies, we took the twins out of the institute yesterday," Tania began the moment she sat down.

"You did? I knew it. I just knew it," Endermo said. "That afternoon I visited you," he said to Tania, "you had already taken them out, right?" She nodded. "And you were on the verge of telling me, weren't you?"

"Yes, but you don't know the reason. It wasn't

just to confess. Alpha did a terrible thing when we took her to see the children. She caused one of them to have an accident."

"Sent an electric shock through the child while he was on the monkey bars," Neil explained. Endermo nodded.

"What happened to the child?"

"He's all right, but he has some broken bones. Of course, we took the twins back immediately."

"Now convinced we were right about Alpha, we snuck into the basement corridor last night and broke into Henderson's office so we could find something concrete to present you," Tania said. "We didn't want to take the chance of Henderson coming up with any other convenient explanations. That's where Neil got that folder."

"What is that folder?"

"It's Henderson's records on the results of his experiments with extrasensory powers, which is the real reason why he's working with the twins and with other birth defective children down in his corridor."

"You mean his monsters?"

"You did know about them, then," Tania said.

"Yes, it was something I reluctantly agreed to, but I thought, to keep a man like Henderson on this project, a project not many would take as seriously . . . it was not that much of a compromise. And, after all, nobody wanted these poor creatures, so . . ."

"You don't know all of it," Neil said quickly. "These aren't malformed children caused by some accidental genetic mix-up, then eagerly surrendered by the distraught parents. These creatures are Henderson's own creations."

"Pardon?"

"You sure this can't bring on some kind of relapse?" Tania asked cautiously.

"No. This heart attack was caused by physical factors, a jolt of electricity to be specific. I survived it and there is no real muscle damage, thank heavens."

"Okay," Neil said. "Here's what we found out." He began to pull out some of the sheets from the folder, explaining as he went along. He showed Endermo the sheet that contained descriptions of the mothers, then he and Tania told Endermo about their visit with Patricia Hooks and what it all meant. Endermo listened quietly, his eyes expressing his outrage and surprise periodically.

"This is what I get for being more of an administrator than a doctor," Endermo said. "You get comfortable in your office pushing papers, taking lunches, talking on phones, and you lose track with what is really happening right under your eyes. It's all my fault."

"You've got to remember the kind of man Henderson is," Neil said. "He lives under his own set of rules, his own version of morality. He moves about here like a phantom, cloaked in his own secrets. No one wants to go down into that basement and no one understands what he's doing. So he goes about on his own, performing his personal horror unchecked."

"I should have been the one to check it," Endermo said. "No excuses. What's important now is we put a stop to it, and we save those twins from any further experimentation and distortion."

"Well, we might have just done that," Neil said. He took out the sheet in the folder that had the New Jersey telephone number and reference code on it, and told Dr. Endermo about his phone call.

"I know what you hoped to accomplish," Endermo said. "But I don't think that's going to work. Even if they took the twins out and Henderson closed down his laboratory in the basement, we could not be sure he wasn't moving it all, lock, stock, and barrel to another institution they found for him."

"That's right, Neil," Tania said. "We should have thought of that."

"As long as he has Alpha and Beta and can demonstrate her powers, he'll get certain government types to move mountains for him."

"Well . . . what do we do about him?"

"I called you here, even without knowing about some of these other things because I wanted you to get them away from Dr. Henderson.

"I had a suspicion," he said, smiling at Tania, "that you two had already met with some success getting the twins out when you wanted to, so I thought you should do it again."

"Get them out? And then what? Bring them to the media and expose what Henderson has done?"

"No, Neil. I still feel that would do them more

damage than good, and with the added aspect of Alpha's extrasensory powers . . ."

"They would become even more freaky," Tania said.

"Exactly. No, I have already contacted someone who will take them and place them in a program designed the way ours was supposed to be, sans Henderson," Endermo said. "I want you to bring the twins to him. Tonight. Tania, in that drawer . . ." Endermo indicated the small nightstand. She opened the drawer and took out an index card. On it was a name and an address in Princeton, New Jersey.

"Dr. Anthony Fulton?"

"He's a colleague, someone we can trust, and someone who knows about the twins already. Everything's being prepared for their eventual arrival." Endermo sat up a bit and gripped Neil's right wrist. "Neil, you've got to get them out and away from Henderson. Without them he's just another bizarre scientist. He won't be able to manipulate anyone, especially the government types who finance his crazy projects, and . . . most of all . . . you'll do what's most humane for the twins."

"Yes, he's right," Tania said quickly. "Neil?"

"Okay, but it's going to be a lot harder getting them out now than it was yesterday. I made that call and Henderson is on to us."

"I've taken care of some of that. I have already spoken to the head of my security. He knows you two are coming into the institute tonight. No one will prevent you from getting to the twins' apartment, no matter what Henderson tells them. My orders are clear; no one can supersede them."

"But the thing is," Tania said softly, looking first at Neil, then at Dr. Endermo, "will Alpha permit us to help her and Beta?"

Endermo lowered himself to the pillow again.

"That's why I wanted you two," he said. "I'm sure she'll trust you more than she would anyone else. In fact, without Henderson, you're probably the only people who could get her to agree."

They both stared at him. He suddenly looked tired and pale.

"I'm sorry," he said. "Sorry, that something so interesting and wonderful in many ways has turned out to be so distasteful and dangerous. I won't blame you if you just want to walk away."

"We can't do that," Neil said. He stood up.

"No, we can't," Tania said, rising.

Dr. Endermo turned to them, the smile returning.

"I thought you two would feel that way. I wish I could go along with you, but in the circumstances . . ."

"That's all right. You just recuperate. We're going to need your help afterward to drive the last nail into Henderson's coffin," Neil said. Endermo nodded and looked at the folder.

"Did you make copies of that?"

"No. I didn't think of it and the way we've been going . . ."

"I'd like to read all of it, but we should have

another copy. Wait a minute." He pushed his buzzer and the CCU nurse returned. "Lucy, I need a favor," he said.

"Now Dr. Endermo, you were only supposed to . . ."

"I'm not going to do anything," he said quickly. "Could you have this folder xeroxed immediately and have the copy placed in the hospital safe for me."

The nurse nodded.

"All right," she said. "I'll do it."

"Thank you, Lucy."

"But I really think you two have been here long enough, though," she said to Neil and Tania. She took the folder and walked out, her heels clicking. Neil watched her for a moment, distracted by the sound, then looked at Endermo. He seemed more relaxed.

"You guys can do this," he said. "And help end this nightmare."

"We'll try," Neil said.

"Feel better," Tania said. "We'll contact you as soon as we have the twins safely out of here."

"Good." He closed his eyes. "Thank you."

They left quickly. In the elevator on the way down, Neil took her hand and smiled.

"Well, Dr. Weber," he said, "if we ever needed your expertise as a psychologist, we're going to need it tonight when we enter that apartment and confront Alpha, so bone up on all your persuasive techniques."

"Is that so, Mr. Richards? Well, you had just

better review every technique you've ever used as a special education teacher, too."

Neil nodded. They went back through the lobby and returned the CCU pass to the pink lady, who leaned over to whisper something to him before he left the desk.

"Yes?"

"Very attractive young lady," she said, hoping he would reveal some tidbit of gossip for her to carry into the community. He looked at Tania as though first noticing her.

"Why, yes. I hadn't noticed. Thank you for pointing that out," he said and left her, mouth agape.

"What did she say?" Tania asked as they walked out the door and headed for the parking lot.

"She asked me if you were my girlfriend."

"She didn't. What nerve some people have." After a pause, she added, "And what did you say?"

"The truth. I said no."

"What?"

"I said you were my fiancée." She laughed and took his arm. "Now don't go and make me out to be a liar," he added and opened the car door for her. She stared at him a moment, then smiled.

"No chance of that," she said.

They drove off to rest at his apartment until the time came to rescue the twins.

12

Shortly after they arrived at Neil's apartment, Tania called the number Dr. Endermo had given her and spoke to Dr. Anthony Fulton. She found him rather businesslike and to the point. He had been expecting their call and needed no introductions. Arrangements were made for a rendezvous only a few miles away once they had taken the twins out of the institute. Fulton called it "the exchange."

"I felt like I was talking about sneaking spies across borders or something. Such intrigue," she told Neil, who had finally taken his shower and had come out with one towel wrapped around his waist and one around his neck.

"Maybe melodramatic, but necessary, I suppose. Hungry?"

"Hadn't thought about it until you just asked," she said. "But, now that you did . . ."

"Let me slip into something," he replied, slapping his hands together, "and I'll whip up some chicken and cashews in the wok. Gives me the chance to show off my culinary skills."

"I'm too nervous to just sit around and wait while you do it all."

"Set the table; put up some rice. You'll find it in the cabinet over the sink."

They were both grateful for the opportunity to digress, to think about other things, to act as though their lives were normal and uncomplicated. They chatted with a nervous energy characteristic of two people brought together for the very first time, relating how it was to live alone, recalling the most insignificant experiences and describing them as though they were each traumatic events. It became obvious that they were trying to prevent any moments of silence.

"This is really very good," she said, serving herself a second helping.

"Survival skills for the eighties. Either you become a good cook or live off TV dinners and like fare."

They laughed, and there was finally a long, silent pause. Tania glanced at the clock.

"It doesn't get dark until nearly eight-thirty now," Neil said softly. He put his hand over hers affectionately. "We've got time."

"I know, but I wish it would go fast and we'd get it over with, don't you?"

"Of course."

She sat back.

"You know what I was thinking about while you were getting dressed? What are we going to do afterward?"

"Afterward?"

"Once the twins are gone?"

Neil stared at her a moment.

"You know, I never gave that a thought, but you're right. What are we going to do afterward? We've eliminated our own jobs." She shook her head, then they both laughed.

"I guess I can speak to Dr. Forster and under the circumstances, get my job back. And as for you . . . they're always looking for a good school psychologist around here. Feel free to use me as a reference."

"Thanks," she said, then turned serious again. "Let's just take it one step at a time." He nodded.

"Coffee? We have time," he added.

"Okay. Why don't you let me make that and let me take care of cleaning up."

"Well . . ."

"I'll guarantee you a dispensation from women's lib."

"Okay, since you put it that way, I'll pretend to be a pre-sixties male chauvinist pig and go into the living room to watch the news while you slave over the sink." He got up and kissed her. "It's going to be all right," he said. "We'll put this off and clean up this mess."

"Sure we will. I'm all right. Go on."

Neil watched the news until Tania served coffee in the living room, then they finally permitted themselves to talk about how they would go about taking the twins out.

"I'll park just where I parked when we took them out to bring them to the school. We'll take them down through the same exit. I'll back the car up. We'll get them in and be off. Just as simple as it was before."

"But what are we going to tell them this time, Neil? Alpha is sure to see through us if we fabricate some excuses."

"That's why I thought we would just tell them the truth, confront them with what Henderson is doing and tell them his eventual plans for them. Surely Alpha won't want to see Beta destroyed. When they realize Dr. Endermo has sent us and they see how intent we are on saving them and ending the horror . . ."

"And Alpha finally hears us say she was right . . . there are others like her and Beta . . ."

"She should be cooperative."

"In a real sense we've become dependent upon her power to read our true thoughts, to be perceptive. Hopefully, she *will* know that we are on their side."

"If Henderson hasn't turned them against us already, somehow," Neil said. He looked sharply at her. "We've got to consider that possibility, Tania. If we see we won't be able to do this, we'll have to effect an immediate retreat. I'll say something like, 'All right, we'll come back to discuss this tomorrow,' and then we'll head for the door, okay?"

"Okay." she said. He looked at his watch. She picked up the coffee cups and saucers and went out to the kitchen. When she returned, he was waiting in the doorway.

"Ready?"

"Yes."

"We can still back out of this. Tell Endermo to find some other way."

"From a hospital bed in CCU? He's hardly in a position to do battle with Dr. Henderson. No, this is the best way. I'll be all right. They're just an unusual pair of twins."

"Sure. Just your typical conjoined twins with extrasensory powers manipulated by a mad scientist," he said and they smiled. He took her hand. "We're off."

They slipped out of his apartment and entered his car as quietly as two shadows.

"After we get them to agree to go, you get a blanket from their bedroom," Neil said.

"They might not be dressed. Sometimes by this time, they're dressed for bed."

"We'll take them out in whatever they're in. I'm sure their needs will be provided for at the next place."

Tania nodded. They said nothing else during the trip to the institute. He slowed down when he reached the main gate. Now that night had fallen, the structure and its surroundings took on that same eerie glow Neil recalled from the night before. They entered and found the parking lot by the research center just as deserted and just as quiet.

"Don't see Henderson's car anywhere," Tania said as he pulled into the lot.

After they parked and Neil shut off the engine, they sat there for a few moments studying the entrances, searching the long, deep shadows, watching for any movement, waiting for any sound. All was deadly quiet and deadly still.

"Looks good," Neil said. "Let's go."

They got out of the car and walked to the side entrance they usually took. Both of them were conscious of their footsteps by the echo through the darkness, reverberating off the stone structure. For a moment Neil had the image of the nurse in the basement flash before him. He recalled the clicking sound of her footsteps, how they sounded like the tapping of a small hammer, and then, for some reason, he thought about the clicking of the nurse's footsteps in CCU. The image lingered, then disappeared like rising smoke. The deep silence in and around the hospital and the institute had always unnerved him and made him conscious of every sound, no matter how small. He realized that was why he was thinking of these things.

He looked back once, then reached for the door and opened it. Tania stepped in and he quickly followed. The corridor was as quiet as ever, the lights dimmed to a nighttime setting. They hesitated and listened. Not a door opened; not a voice was heard. *Where were the security guards?* he wondered, then thought Dr. Endermo had probably had them pulled off or pulled back to make for a clear escape. No one stood between them and the door to the twins' apartment. He looked at Tania, nodded, then took her hand. They went forward.

They only slowed down when they reached Dr. Endermo's office. There were no lights on and the door was shut. As they continued on, both felt their hearts pound. Tania opened her pocketbook and took out the key that opened the outer door. They paused to look up and down the corridor one more time. Then Neil nodded and Tania inserted the key. She turned it and they heard the small click. Neil put his hand on the knob and opened the door. He felt the beads of sweat thicken over his forehead and begin to run down his temples. Tania looked flushed, her eyes bright with terror. He nodded toward the apartment door and they entered the outer chamber.

"Hope they're not asleep," he whispered.

"They usually watch television now."

He listened before opening the door, but didn't hear the sound of the set.

"Maybe we ought to go into the observation room and check them out first," he said. "Maybe they're not even there; maybe Henderson's moved them into the basement, anticipating something like this."

"Neil," she said, putting her hand on his wrist to calm him. "Alpha will sense us spying on her if we go in there and that might cloud her vision and turn her against us before we even start."

"Right," he said. "If they're not there, they're not there. Okay, here we go," he said and opened the door.

Although the television set was off, the twins sat on the couch staring at the dark screen. They wore their specially made cream-and-pink nightgown and pink slippers. Both girls had their hair loose and brushed down. Beta turned when Neil opened the door, but snapped her head back so sharply it looked as if it was connected to her neck by some small but powerful spring. Alpha never moved.

Tania reached out to press her hand into Neil's. They looked at one another, then entered the apartment. Alpha didn't look at them until they were actually standing before her and Beta.

"Alpha," Neil said, deciding he would direct himself specifically to her since she had all the power and control anyway. "We've come to take you and Beta out of here. For good," he added. He thought he detected some satisfaction in Beta's eyes. She looked quickly at Alpha.

Alpha's eyes narrowed. Her face appeared carved out of ice. Her lips were so still. Neil thought she looked as if she were in an hypnotic state. Beta's face was far more animated, her eyes wider, her lips quivering. A part of her wanted to smile and a part of her prevented it.

"Miss Weber and I have discovered that some terrible things are being done here, Alpha, and we discovered that terrible things will be done to you and Beta," he continued.

Suddenly, as if those words were the cue, speakers from the observation room to the apartment were turned on. The loud, metallic click made Alpha's eyelids flutter. Tania squeezed Neil's hand harder and they both looked up when Dr. Endermo's voice came through.

"Good evening, Neil, Tania. Glad you could make it."

"Dr. Endermo?" Tania said. Both she and Neil turned toward the one-way mirror. "Is that you?"

"Of course, my dear."

"You were released from CCU? You've come to help?" she asked.

"Yes," he said. "I've come to help. Actually, I've come to be more of an observer. I think you two will appreciate this." His tone of voice changed, obviously because he had turned to someone else. "Why don't we eliminate the mirror now. There's no longer any need."

"Fine," Dr. Henderson replied and a switch was thrown. Instantly the mirror became a large window through which Neil and Tania could see Sanford Endermo, now dressed in a suit and tie, standing next to Dr. Henderson, still wearing his long lab coat. Seated beside them were three other men, none of whom Tania or Neil knew. They were all dressed in business suits and sat with that same detached interest characteristic of a man like Henderson.

Dr. Endermo no longer looked sick and weak. He appeared to be his old self, that same wide smile, that relaxed posture.

"What's going on here?" Neil asked, not that he really had to. All of it was spinning out quickly . . . Endermo had staged his own heart attack and placed himself in CCU just so he could win their complete confidence. As soon as Henderson had realized his secret file was missing, he must have got right to him and they planned out the ruse. *And we gave him back the file*, Neil thought. *Willingly.*

"I'm sure you two very intelligent people have figured most of it out by now."

"You were in on it all," Tania said. "You lied to us."

"Had to do what was necessary to protect the project, Tania. Something like this is bigger than a few individuals. Dr. Henderson has really done remarkable work with the twins and with his ancillary experimentation. We are on the brink of making some rather wonderful discoveries about the human mind and its potential. In some ways this is more exciting than the discovery of the atom and the subsequent achievement of nuclear energy, although it's been a little unpredictable at times, right, Neil? Remember that first day when I received a small shock? But Tania has done remarkable work. Alpha's a lot more even-tempered. We think we have things under control now."

"Let's get on with it," Henderson interjected curtly.

"Yes, of course. I'm afraid Dr. Henderson doesn't have the patience for social intercourse. But that's something you two always knew and complained about. To each other," he added.

"You had my office bugged?" Tania said, realizing the implication.

"Of course," Endermo said.

"So you always knew what we knew?"

"Exactly."

"Well, why did you let it go on?" Neil asked. "Why didn't you stop us earlier?"

"We had our reasons. Actually, you two were part of an overall experiment involving the twins. And we needed your expertise in your individual fields. If you weren't so perceptive and didn't go ahead investigating areas you shouldn't have been in, we might have been able to continue this relationship. You two would have earned nice wages and had the experiences you wanted. But alas, curiosity, morality, whatever you want to call it, got in the way. As much as it pains me to say it, however, you will be replaced easily enough."

"You're crazy. You're all crazy," Neil said. The three seated men remained unmoving, as indifferent as mannequins. Henderson, however, was fidgety.

"Sanford," he said.

"All right."

"We're leaving. And we're taking the twins out with us," Neil said. Endermo laughed.

"You don't understand, do you? Why do you think I arranged for you two to come here tonight and made it so easy for you to do so? We wanted you in the twins' apartment. It's all part of our experimentation. These gentlemen beside me have come to see how their investment is paying off."

"Alpha," Neil said, turning back to the twins, "you've got to get yourself and Beta out of here with us. You heard him—they're doing experiments on you. We know how those experiments are going to end up."

"Alpha," Henderson suddenly said. "Concentrate on them."

Alpha's head turned in tiny increments until she faced both of them squarely.

"Neil," Tania said. "Look at her. It's no use."

Neil looked at her, then at Endermo and Henderson.

"Okay. Let's leave," he said. He turned and they headed for the door. Fortunately, he released Tania's hand just before he grasped the handle. The shock was a great deal stronger than the one Endermo had suffered. For a few moments, he couldn't let go of the metal. His fingers were on fire and the flames traveled up through his arm and into his shoulder. He fell back with a scream and dropped to the floor. Tania screamed and put her hands over her face instinctively. Neil rolled about, rubbing his arm and shoulder. Finally, he caught his breath.

"I'm all right," he said looking up at Tania. "I'm all right."

She took her hands from her face and looked back at the twins. Beta's eyes were nearly shut—she swayed slightly—but Alpha was erect, her eyes wide, her mouth pulled back at the corners in a terrible grimace. She looked like an angry dog.

"Neil, how will we get out of here?" Tania asked. Neil sat up and looked about the room. There was no other exit but the door. His arm hung limply at his side. He opened and closed his fist to bring back a surge of blood.

"Alpha," Henderson commanded. "Place the picture."

"Now you'll see something," Neil heard Dr. Endermo say. He looked at the twins and found himself drawn to Alpha's eyes. He thought about bringing his left hand up to cover his own eyes, but he never got his hand off the floor.

When he turned back to Tania, he no longer saw her. Instead, he saw Dr. Henderson, the man responsible for all this, the man who created those double monsters downstairs in the basement, the man who had turned Alpha into a terrible creature, the man who now had placed him and Tania into a life-threatening situation. It was going to be him or them.

"Neil?" Tania said. The look on Neil's face had changed so radically. She saw the anger and hate and now the determination. She looked back at the twins. Alpha was still staring at Neil, concentrating. Beta's eyes were completely shut.

Neil rose to his feet.

"Neil?"

His hands were clenched into fists. She backed up a few steps and looked at the large window. Endermo and Henderson were right up against it, both their faces bright with anticipation. The three men were sitting forward now, their faces finally animated. They looked like baseball fans at some stadium.

Neil stepped toward her.

"You bastard," he said.

"Oh no," Tania said. "No, Neil. It's me. No. Oh, God, no," she said looking for an avenue of escape.

She couldn't go to the door. "Alpha, stop!" she screamed.

"Stop telling her to do things," Neil said. It was now clear to Tania that he saw Henderson and not her and heard things Henderson would say and not what she was really saying.

"Oh Neil, I'm not telling her things. I'm not Henderson. Fight it, fight it!" she pleaded. He continued toward her aggressively. She retreated until she had her back against the wall.

"Now what is occurring," Henderson explained calmly, "is not really mesmerism. He is not being hypnotized in the old-fashioned sense. What Alpha is doing is interfering with the message his eyes are bringing to his brain. Those messages are being intercepted, if you like, and replaced with images already locked in memory. She is, in effect, stimulating a dream. He will only see me, and as he kills her, he will believe he is killing me."

"*Alpha!*" Tania screamed. Neil lunged for her. She blocked his hand with her forearm and sidestepped, then rushed across the room until she was in front of Alpha.

"Get away from them!" Neil commanded. "You've done enough harm to those poor creatures."

"Alpha," she said, ignoring him. "You must not do this. You're going to hurt Mr. Richards and me. We're here to help you. Please, Alpha. Try to listen to me. You were right," she pleaded. "There are others like you. You were right."

"Get away from her," Neil snarled. He came toward her again.

"Neil! Stop!"

"Bastard," Neil said. He clutched the table lamp like a club and raised it as he came forward.

"Alpha!" Tania cried. "They're going to destroy Beta. They're going to cut her away and keep you in a wheelchair. Please listen to me."

Alpha blinked.

Neil lunged forward and swung the lamp. Tania pushed herself back, but she didn't fall completely clear. The bottom of the lamp struck her in the shoulder and she screamed and fell to the floor. Neil stood over her, his face distorted, his eyes wild, his mouth twisted.

"Alpha, listen. Look into Neil's mind. Read his true thoughts. We know what they're going to do to you. See for yourself," she pleaded. Alpha blinked again. Neil brought the lamp up.

Tania turned on her side as he brought it down, smashing it on the floor just beside her head.

"Alpha! They're going to cut Beta away!" she screamed; they were her last clear words. Neil straddled her and seized her throat. She grasped his wrists and tried desperately to pull his fingers off, but his hands had become a steel collar closing tighter and tighter. She felt the blood drain from her face.

Just before she went unconscious, she vaguely felt the loosening of his fingers.

Neil snapped into an erect sitting position. It was as if someone had grabbed the back of his head and pulled him up by the hairs; there was that much pain across his temples and forehead.

"Alpha!" Henderson screamed over the speakers. "Continue the pictures!"

Neil looked at Alpha. Her eyes were wider. He could almost feel her in his head, scanning his thoughts, reading his memory, quickly turning the pages of all his recent experiences and skimming them like a copying machine. He couldn't move; she held him firmly in place.

"Alpha!" Henderson screamed.

"What's happening?" Dr. Endermo asked, his voice now filled with concern.

"She's stepped out of the command," Henderson said. "Damn it."

"What does this mean?" one of the men beside Endermo inquired. Henderson didn't reply.

"Alpha, listen to my voice and my voice only," Henderson said.

Alpha turned very slowly toward the window. Her eyes narrowed again.

"What is it?" Dr. Endermo asked. He stepped back instinctively. Alpha's face was flushed.

"She's read his mind," Henderson said. "She knows."

"Gentlemen," Endermo said. "Perhaps we . . ."

The glass partition shattered as if some huge boulder had been heaved into the center of it. All the glass fell inward toward Henderson, Endermo, and the three men. They screamed and rushed for the door. The first man who touched the handle howled in pain. His entire body shook. The others backed away. When he released his grip on the handle, he drew his arm up over his head as if he wanted to throw it from his body. Then he fell backward, falling into the shattered glass.

"*Alpha, sleep!*" Henderson commanded. "*Sleep!*"

Alpha and Beta rose from the couch, Beta's eyes still closed. They turned completely toward the observation room.

"*Alpha, no!*" Henderson screamed.

There was an explosion. The room burst into flames, fire coming from the floor and from the walls. A ribbon of blue flame even broke out across the ceiling, looking like a long, neon bulb. Whatever glass remained on the frame fell inward, a long sliver slicing across Dr. Endermo's neck. Blood gushed over his suit and even shot up onto his face. He clutched his neck and fell forward, falling into the apartment. Henderson rushed forward, seeing that as an avenue of escape, but he bounced back as if he had struck an invisible wall and fell over the flames that were almost as tall as him. His screams joined the screams of the remaining two men, all of it now becoming a chorus of final pleas and cries as the fire continued to torture and consume their bodies.

Neil blinked rapidly and looked down at Tania's unconscious form beneath him. The fire was extending beyond the observation room, moving in their direction. He shook her once, then knelt down, slipped his arms under her, and lifted her as he stood.

"Alpha," he cried. "Follow me out!"

She turned and looked at him; her face had changed dramatically. Gone was the hard, cold look. She looked more like Beta, who remained asleep. A chunk of the wall on the left fell toward them; the flaming material struck the back of the couch, which instantly burst into flames. Neil jerked back. Alpha and Beta followed.

"Quickly," he said, and headed for the door. When he stepped out into the corridor, he heard alarms ringing. People were shouting and rushing toward them. He moved down the hallway away from the fire. A maintenance man came up beside him, followed by two security guards.

"What the hell happened?" the maintenance man asked. The security guards had fire extinguishers in their hands. They went directly to the observation room door and began spraying, but the flames were far too large for them to be effective.

"Get the twins out!" Neil shouted and carried Tania farther down the hall. He set her down by the bathroom door and rushed in for wet towels. When he came out, she was stirring. He placed a towel over her forehead and dabbed her cheeks with another until she opened her eyes.

"Neil?"

Fear was clearly still written in her face.

"It's all right; it's all right. Alpha snapped out of it. She saw what we knew and she turned on them. The place is on fire," he said. More people were rushing about now.

"The twins?" Tania asked.

He turned back and looked toward their apartment. The entire wall was a red and yellow wall of flame. People were retreating.

"I don't know," he said. "We've got to get out of here. Can you stand?"

"Yes."

He helped her to her feet and they made their way out of the institution. The sound of the first fire engine could be heard in the distance. People were running and shouting everywhere. Tania stumbled in the parking lot. He felt how weak she was and held her closely to him. Suddenly, she passed out again. One of the interns from the hospital spotted them and came to his assistance.

"Let's get her to the emergency room," the intern said.

Neil lifted her into his arms again and carried her most of the way. The intern rushed ahead and got a stretcher. They placed her on it and rolled her into the emergency room.

"What happened to her neck?" he asked as soon as they had her in one of the examination rooms. Her skin was burned with the shape of Neil's fingers. He shook his head.

"I don't know; I'm not sure."

"Looks like she was choked."

The emergency room doctor appeared and they brought her back to a conscious state rapidly. While they worked on her, Neil went to the emergency room door to see the fire engine arrive and go around to the institute parking lot. Moments later another fire engine arrived, then another.

He came back in as the emergency room doctor came out of the examination room.

"She'll be all right," he said, "but I've given her a sedative."

Neil nodded. He saw the emergency room doctor start to say something else, but he never heard a word.

Suddenly, all went blank for him, too. And like a suit jacket that had slipped off its hanger, he folded up at the doctor's feet.

13

The twins were never found. It was as though the fire knew where to travel to purge the world of Henderson's work. By the time the first fire truck arrived and set up, the conflagration had spread throughout the research institute. The fire department was successful, however, in cutting it off from the hospital proper. Even though patients and personnel were never in any danger, a partial evacuation had been carried out.

Neil regained consciousness in the emergency room. The doctor examined him but could determine nothing physically wrong. They suggested he remain under observation at least overnight and he, too, was given a sedative. Hours later, both he and Tania awoke in separate hospital rooms on the third floor. The nurses quickly saw that he wasn't going to remain there unless he could reassure himself that Tania was all right. They took him down to see her and left the two of them alone for a while.

"Hi," he said. He moved a chair to the side of her bed and took her hand. She smiled weakly; the after-effects of the ordeal still clearly embroidered in her face. She was lying back, the bed having been raised so she could see and speak to him comfortably. She was dressed in a hospital gown, as was he, only she had a light gauze bandage around her neck as well.

"Hi. Why are you in a hospital gown, too?"

"Apparently I passed out soon after you were treated. Guess I was mentally exhausted. The doctor asked me to stay just as a precaution. They thought it was all a result of being caught in the fire. I wasn't up to describing everything that had happened and thought it was best simply to take a rest. I feel a bit washed out."

"It's no wonder."

"Does that hurt?" he asked, indicating her neck.

"It's sore. I have a little trouble swallowing, but the doctor said it will ease off considerably by tomorrow."

"I did that, didn't I?" He nodded, answering his own question, his face glum.

"No. Henderson did it through you," she said.

"Thanks."

"It's true. You, of all people, should know that."

"Still, I feel as though I should have been able to prevent it."

"You weren't doing it to me. You thought you were doing it to Henderson. It doesn't matter, Neil. That part is over, thank God. What have they discovered since we've been here? Have you learned anything?"

"The nurses gave me some information. They

found the five bodies in the observation room, all five burned beyond recognition. The institute is a total disaster, floors and walls caved in; so much destroyed, it's hard to tell what was what apparently."

"What about the twins?"

"Well, of course the nurses here know nothing about them. The firemen are still combing through the rubble, but it looks like they didn't get to them in time, even though no one's discovered the remains of any children. Maybe . . . maybe it's for the best."

"So as of now, people don't know what really went on in there?"

"Not from what I've been told. As soon as you're strong enough, we'll go see the hospital administrator."

"I'll be all right in the morning. I'm just so tired."

"Sure. I'm not exactly a ball of fire myself." He stared at her a moment. "If I would have . . ."

"Neil, stop thinking about it. If I can deal with it, you certainly should be able to also."

"Unfair analogy. You're a psychologist."

"I'm also a woman."

"I've noticed." He leaned over to kiss her just as the nurse returned to fetch him.

In the morning they were both refreshed and rested enough to be released. Tania still wore a gauze bandage about her throat. Neil had immediately asked for a meeting with Robert Masterson, the chief administrator of the Mandicott Clinic, so as soon as they left the hospital business office, they went directly to Masterson's office.

They found Masterson to be in his mid-thirties, younger than they would have imagined. He had known vaguely about Tania and knew nothing about Neil. As soon as they sat down, they began to relate all that had gone on in the research complex. Masterson, a man about six feet tall, with light, brown hair and youthful, hazel eyes, listened politely, nodding after everything they said as though he agreed or knew. But when they concluded with a description of what finally had happened in the twins' apartment, his eyes widened and he smiled skeptically.

"Of course, I knew Dr. Endermo well," he said in a calm, even tone of voice, "but I had little to do with Dr. Henderson."

"He liked to keep things that way," Neil said. "For what are obvious reasons now."

"Uh huh. Well, of course, we're still going through the debris, but as of now, I have no reports about any nursery filled with . . . what did you call them? Double monsters?"

"Yes," Tania said. "It's actually a clinical term, although I was never comfortable with it."

"This is incredible."

"Then you knew absolutely nothing about it?" Neil asked.

"I knew Dr. Endermo was working on some well-kept secret project, but I just assumed it was being kept secret for the obvious reasons . . . to prevent spies from other hospitals and drug companies from stealing their research. You have to understand," he said, leaning forward quickly, "that part of the clinic was built and maintained with funds from other government agencies. My main concern was only to keep things smooth between the two areas . . . parking, security, utilities, etc."

"So what you're telling us now is that you knew nothing about it and no one has discovered anything in the remains that relates to what we've described?" Neil concluded.

"That's it in a nutshell," Masterson said. He sat back. "I've got enough problems of my own just in the hospital. I wasn't going over there to poke my nose into their affairs and bring on more problems for myself. We've got a labor dispute with the hospital workers union going. There might be a strike," he added.

It was obvious from the way he went on and on about his administrative problems that Masterson not only did not give much credence to their tale, but he wasn't going to instigate any investigation either. Another government agency would handle the clean-up of the research institute.

Frustrated and tired, they left Masterson's office and drove back to Tania's apartment. For a while they simply sat around, wondering what else they could do about it all. They had no concrete evidence to present to the media; they knew no one else to call or see.

In the end they decided to pull their lives together. Neil went to see Dr. Forster and, without going into the sordid details, told him his work ended with the fire at the institute. The school superintendent was happy to have him return to work in the fall. He hadn't even hired a replacement yet.

Tania applied to some of the area schools and received an appointment to a position in an adjacent school district. Their relationship grew stronger. They became engaged in the fall, just after school had begun, and were married right before the Christmas holiday so they could use the vacation period for a honeymoon. They set up house in a modest, three-bedroom, ranch-style home they rented just outside of Centerville, and by the last quarter of the school year, Tania became pregnant.

Even though neither said so to the other, they were both terrified of the possibility of having twins. Early on, however, their doctor assured them that wasn't the case. Tania's pregnancy proceeded without a hitch; she took her vitamins, exercised and ate properly, and visited the doctor regularly. One night at the beginning of her eighth month, they received a rather strange phone call.

Although they had promised one another that they would try not to bring their work home, the nature of both their jobs made it difficult, if not impossible to do so. Tania often received calls at night from social workers, truant officers, and parents; and Neil occasionally described one of his students and sought Tania's advice.

So when the phone rang and the woman on the other end identified herself as a private nurse working in a mental institution just outside of New

York City, Neil assumed it had something to do with one of Tania's cases. He was curious, however, because the nurse asked to speak with Miss Weber, and Tania had stopped using her maiden name the day they were married.

"Who is it?" she asked, getting up from the couch. He often teased her now about the way she wobbled and twisted. She was carrying low and looked like a woman more in the final week of her ninth month instead of just starting the eighth.

"Mrs. Lucy, a private nurse at the Crystal Lake Hospital for the Mentally Disabled. Asking for Miss Weber."

"Huh?" He shrugged and handed her the phone. "Yes," she said, "this is Mrs. Richards, formerly Miss Weber."

He stood by while she listened. Her face reddened.

"What?" he said. She held up her hand and listened some more.

"Yes," she said finally, "we'll be there tomorrow. I know where it is." Without saying goodbye, she cradled the receiver.

"What?" he repeated. She was staring as if in a daze.

"She identified herself as a private nurse, all right, calling on behalf of her patient."

"So?"

"Her patient's name is Beta."

It was a crisp, dry, early December Saturday, a pretty day for traveling, but at breakfast, Neil considered not going.

"With you in the final stages of your pregnancy and all, any sort of emotional excitement . . ."

"I'm fine. I'll be all right. Really."

"Maybe we should just call someone."

"Who? Masterson? The police? The newspapers? We don't even know what this is all about."

"Somehow, they got them out and into a mental institution," Neil conjectured. "But why would they want us to visit them after keeping it a secret so long?"

"You see," Tania said. "Our curiosity would only drive us crazy anyway. We have no choice."

He nodded, reluctantly agreeing.

It was an easy trip, traffic was light. They arrived at Crystal Lake less than an hour-and-a-half later. One of the better run and more plush, private hospitals for the mentally ill, Crystal Lake was located about a mile-and-a-half west of the main highway on a wooded side road that was on the south side of a two-mile-long lake. It wasn't quite frozen over. Sheets of ice floated independently of one another and the houses along the western and northern shores looked closed up and deserted. Neil imagined they were mostly summer homes.

Leafless trees and tall pines stood like sentinels in a still forest surrounding the hospital itself. Neil felt as if he and Tania had slipped into an oil painting. There was no one outside the buildings; no vehicles moved, and the small, puffy clouds looked glued against the azure sky.

"Meditative," he said. "Perfect location for such a place."

Tania said nothing. They had both grown pensive as they had drawn closer to the hospital. Filled with anticipation, she stared ahead. Neil pulled into the visitor's parking lot, his being the only car there now, and turned off the engine, but he didn't move to open the door. Tania looked at him quizzically.

"I don't know if we should do this," he said again.

"Neil, we drove all this way."

"Doesn't matter. This past year we've been able to put it all behind us. To get involved again . . ." He shook his head.

"It was the twins who asked for us, Neil. It must have been them." He nodded, but didn't move. "I'm going in, whether you come or not," she said decisively. "I've got to know."

"Okay."

They got out and walked to the main entrance. The lobby, a large room with a half dozen soft chairs and two couches, was plush. It had a thick, light blue carpet, as many small tables as there were chairs, and racks with magazines alongside chairs and one of the couches. The walls were covered with a dark pine paneling with paintings of country scenes, a large painting of Crystal Lake, and a few portraits of trustees spaced evenly along the center and right walls. It was a well-lit room, illuminated by four large chandeliers.

To the left was the main desk, a long, light pine wood counter, behind which sat an elderly woman dressed in a blue and white uniform. She had her gray hair pinned back and wore a pair of thick glasses. Her face was thin, the features so sharp, she looked somewhat undernourished. She didn't look up until they were nearly to the counter and seemed annoyed by their arrival. There was nothing friendly in her eyes, no warmth, not even a professional, albeit mechanical courtesy characteristic of seasoned receptionists.

"Can I help you?" she asked in a monotone.

"Yes," Tania said. "We are Mr. and Mrs. Richards, here to see Beta."

"Beta?"

"Yes. I was called under my maiden name," Tania explained quickly, imagining that was why the woman seemed confused.

"Weber."

"Called? Who called you?"

"A Mrs. Lucy," Neil said quickly, impatience crawling into his voice immediately.

"You mean Arlene Lucy?"

"She identified herself only as Mrs. Lucy," Tania said. "Why? Is there a problem about this?"

"Just a moment," the woman said. She got up and went through a rear door.

"I hope this wasn't some kind of a joke," Neil said.

A few moments later, the woman reappeared with a younger, but not much taller woman, dressed in a jacket, tie, and skirt. She had a round, somewhat chubby face so that her dark brown eyes looked much smaller and more receded than they were. Creases formed across her wide forehead as she considered Neil and Tania. Her light brown hair was cut just below her ears and hung limply down the sides.

Neil thought she had shoulders that were more like a man's. Her large, maternal bosom pressed her suit jacket open, revealing wide hips as well. The sleeves of her jacket fit a bit too snugly around her puffed upper arms. She wore no makeup and was very fair-skinned with a small patch of freckles under each eye.

"I'm Dr. Thorndike," she said in a deep, but smooth tone of voice, the kind that would sound sexy over the phone. *What a disappointment after someone meets her,* Neil thought. "I'm the chief administrator at Crystal Lake. You say you've come to visit Beta?"

"That's correct," Tania said.

"And Arlene Lucy called you?"

"Yes," Neil said. "Is she not a private nurse here?"

Dr. Thorndike did not reply for a moment. She stared at them.

"I'm sorry if I'm acting a bit confused," she said. "But you see, you people are the first to ever request to see Beta. Beta is a ward of the state, a mentally ill orphan. I understood that she had no family, no friends. She and her sister had been in institutions all their lives, never even being placed in foster homes."

"What about her sister?" Tania asked quickly. Dr. Thorndike looked at Neil, then at Tania, scrutinizing them carefully.

"She's dead. You didn't know that then?"

Neil and Tania looked at one another. Then she turned back to Dr. Thorndike.

"No. How did she die?"

"Horribly. In a fire." She stared at them a moment. "How do you come to know Beta?"

"We were at the last institute in which she resided," Tania said.

"Really?"

"I'm a psychologist and my husband teaches special education."

"Oh, I see. But, surely you two would have known about the fire."

"We knew about it; we just didn't know what had happened to the twins. Surely, you know why," Tania said.

"Well, I . . . no. I don't know why. No one told me I couldn't tell anyone about it, so I don't understand."

"What do you understand?"

"Pardon?"

"Why is Beta here, if I may ask."

"Well, she's suffering from acute schizophrenia since her twin sister's death. At times, she thinks she is her sister and at times, she's herself," Dr. Thorndike said. "It's very sad."

Neither Neil nor Tania responded for a moment.

"Well, who's Arlene Lucy?" Tania asked.

"She is a nurse here assigned to Beta's floor, but . . ."

"Well, she called us," Tania said. "Beta requested it. Is there any reason why we can't see her?"

"No. Of course not. It's just that Mrs. Lucy should have come to me before calling you."

"Well, we've come a long way," Tania said. "You can work out your administrative problem, I'm sure, but in the meantime, we'd appreciate seeing Beta."

"Yes," Dr. Thorndike said. "You're right." She finally smiled. "It might help Beta to see people she once knew. I'll take you to her myself."

"Thank you," Tania said. She and Neil waited for Dr. Thorndike to come around the counter.

"Way to handle the bureaucrats," Neil whispered.

"Right this way," Dr. Thorndike said. They started after her. "She was burned badly in the fire," Dr. Thorndike said, "and spent most of the last year being treated, having skin graft operations . . . all of it terribly traumatic. I suppose you know just how close she and her sister were," she added, turning to them. Tania nearly laughed.

"Close?"

"From what I've been told, they were practically inseparable."

"My God," Tania said. "You really don't know it all, do you?"

"Pardon?"

"Nothing. Please, we'd just like to see her and go."

"I must say, you two are giving me a very bad feeling. I'm very surprised at Arlene Lucy. She's a total professional. This is not like her."

"I'm not surprised," Tania mumbled to herself.

Dr. Thorndike continued down the corridor until they reached the nurses' station. Two nurses were seated at the desk. Both looked up when she approached the counter.

"Arlene?" she said, and the taller nurse with very light brown hair stood up. She had a soft face and looked to be no more than thirty. "This is Mr. and Mrs. Richards." Arlene Lucy smiled quizzically, then looked at Dr. Thorndike. "The people you called," she explained.

"Called?"

"You didn't call these people to request they come visit Beta?"

"Come visit Beta?" The smile left her face, but her blue eyes remained friendly, warm. She had an innocent and compassionate look. Neil thought she would be a prime candidate for mental suggestion.

Dr. Thorndike turned back to Neil and Tania.

"Beta asked you to call us," Tania said. "You called yesterday."

"I'm afraid there's been some mistake."

"Were you on duty about five o'clock yesterday?" Tania demanded quickly.

"Yes, but . . ."

"You called us," she said, nodding. Then she turned to Dr. Thorndike. "How else would we know to come here?" she asked.

"This is all getting very confusing."

"It's not confusing to us, Dr. Thorndike. We're not here to do anything but visit Beta. It will be a short visit. You can come in with us, if you'd like."

"But . . ." She looked at Arlene Lucy, who

raised her eyebrows. "All right," she said. "I've become curious myself as to what Beta's reaction to you two will be. This way," she added, and they continued down the corridor toward the first room on the left.

Dr. Thorndike opened the door. Beta was seated by the window, staring out. She did not turn when the door was opened. Neil and Tania recognized her long, light-brown hair. It was neatly brushed, the strands lying softly as far down as the center of her back. She wore a light gray sweatshirt and a pair of stone-washed jeans with tube socks and tennis sneakers.

"She sits there for hours and hours at a stretch, staring out," Dr. Thorndike whispered. "She seems fascinated with the simplest things . . . cars driving up, birds flitting from tree branch to tree branch, the very sky itself."

"We understand," Tania said, and she and Neil stepped farther into the room.

"Beta," Dr. Thorndike said. "You have visitors."

She turned very slowly and they saw that the left side of her face was scarred and patched with transplanted skin. Her left eyelid drooped some, but the right side of her face seemed untouched. It was as if she were indeed two people, split down the middle.

Tania touched Neil's hand and they moved closer. As Beta confronted them, a smile began to ripple from the right side of her face to the left. Her eyes brightened and she stood up.

"Hi, Beta," Tania said.

"Beta," Neil said.

"You came." She brought her hands together. "Alpha said you would. I didn't believe her, but she said you would for sure. She's always right," she added, looking toward Dr. Thorndike. "About everything."

"Oh, Beta, honey," Tania said. "Sit down. Tell us everything that's happened to you." Tania moved to the second chair and turned it so she could sit and face Beta. Neil stood by her side. Beta looked at Dr. Thorndike again, then sat down.

"What do you want to know?"

"Do you remember the fire?" Neil asked.

"Oh sure. We talk about it every night. And Alpha's not a bit sorry, no matter what happened. Of course," Beta said, looking down, "I tell her that's not right. She should feel sorry, just as she should have felt sorry about the little boy on the monkey bars at the playground, but she's stubborn." She smiled. "You know Alpha."

"Yes," Tania said. "We know Alpha."

"How did you get out of the fire?" Neil asked.

"There was a man—he helped us—and a nurse. They carried us out and put us into an ambulance, then we went to one hospital and another and another until we came here. Are you going to be here now, too?"

"No, honey," Tania said. "We're only here to visit you."

"Alpha said you would come," she repeated.

"Where is Alpha?"

"She's here; she's just not ready to say anything. When she wants to, she will."

"I see. She told Mrs. Lucy, your nurse, to call us, didn't she?"

"Uh huh."

Tania looked at Dr. Thorndike, who simply shrugged.

"I like sitting here by the window," Beta said. "This is the first place where we have a window. Sometimes they take us out for walks and we can sit under the tree out there or play ping pong with Morris."

"Morris?"

"Morris Rosefield," Dr. Thorndike said. "A manic depressive at the end of the hall. He's only nineteen, but he attempted suicide twice."

"Alpha can make him happy whenever she wants him to be happy," Beta said. "Otherwise, he wouldn't want to go out and play with us."

"He *has* improved some since they arrived," Dr. Thorndike said. "I mean, since Beta arrived." She smiled and shook her head. "Sometimes she is so convincing, I forget what I'm doing here."

"We understand," Tania said. "More than you can imagine." She turned back to Beta. "So Alpha is still with you. No matter what they did, they couldn't separate the two of you."

"Oh no, never. We'll never separate. Alpha promised, right, Alpha?"

Beta held her smile for a moment, then a remarkable thing happened. Her face shifted so that the left side seemed more dominant. The smile left and her mouth curled slightly at the corners. Something happened to her eyes, the light and bright warmth was replaced with what both Neil and Tania remembered to be Alpha's coldly penetrating stare. Even Dr. Thorndike was impressed. She took a few steps closer.

"And Dr. Henderson and Dr. Endermo?"

"They're both dead," Tania said. Her voice was breathy, low.

"Good."

"What has happened to you . . . Alpha?" Tania asked. Dr. Thorndike's eyes widened.

"They took away my body, but I knew they were going to do it, so I slipped out before they cut and joined with Beta. Now we share her body and her mind."

"And you can speak to one another?"

"Of course."

"But as long as you do this, everyone will think Beta is sick."

"It doesn't matter what they think," she said, turning to Dr. Thorndike. "We're happy here. It's all right."

"Why did you send for us?" Tania asked.

"To find out what happened and . . ."

"What else?"

"Beta wanted to know you were all right. She doesn't stop asking and wondering, so I thought if you came, she would shut up about it."

"And you? Didn't you wonder?"

"Of course not," she said.

"Why not?" Neil asked quickly.

She smiled widely.

"Because I already knew. Beta just wouldn't believe me. Now she will. You're having a baby soon, I see."

"Yes," Tania said. "Next month."

They stared at one another.

"I know what it is. Do you want me to tell you?"

"No," Tania said quickly. She threaded her arm under Neil's and drew him closer. "We want it to be a surprise. Sometimes surprises, not knowing, can be more fun."

Alpha's smile dissipated. She turned away and looked out the window.

"Alpha?"

She turned back and Beta's face had returned.

"She doesn't want to talk any more," she said. "Will you come back with your baby some day?"

"Would you like that?"

"Yes, oh yes."

"Then we will. Do you think Alpha would like that?"

"She wanted me to ask," Beta said, and both Neil and Tania smiled.

Then Tania stepped forward and kissed her on the right cheek. Beta brought her hand to it to touch the spot. Tania started back, stopped, and leaned forward again to kiss her on the left cheek.

"Goodbye girls," she said. "We'll come back to see you again."

"'Bye," Neil said. "Don't stop reading books and learning things."

They walked to the door. Dr. Thorndike stood

with a look of total confusion and amazement on her face. She followed them as they started out. In the doorway, Neil and Tania turned to look back one more time.

And in the face that stared out at them, they were positive they saw both girls.